THE OFF-BRAND CRIMINALS

KESHAV N

Made with ♥ on the Notion Press Platform
www.notionpress.com

Contents

The Foreground

CHAPTER I

The Discovery

October 16, 2007

As the tires of the truck screeched through the dry sand, the man asleep jolted from his chair with a heavy-eyed face. It was 11:50 at night. Two drunk men occupied the truck cabin wearing wrinkled suits, seemingly tired from a long day of work. They were Cody Mills and Devon Ledger. The vehicle was running low on gas, but they couldn't care less. All they wanted was to somehow escort the truck into the compound. I'm Cody.

He was John, the security manager. Riled up over his head, John looked towards me. He rubbed his balding head, dragging the heavy wooden chair along the floor. A man full of himself in his sixties, John believed he held the most important of all jobs.

We'd ridden the truck to my place. With burglary and hold-ups being an everyday occurrence, it meant no place for families. Not half as happening as downtown Cleveland, I lived right in the middle of a breeding ground for illegal jobs. This housing complex on East Cleveland meant home to me and a few other money-hungry blue and white collars. No one here knew who lived next door.

Dawns were sunny and bright. But when it got to night, the place turned so quiet only to be interrupted by crickets creaking. A lonely building was oddly built on an endless stretch of wastelands, towards a direction no particular, without, what they call, an architectural sense. High walls surrounded the building from all sides save the only entry point: the barred gate — with rusted old rails — outside which we waited. The half-drawn graffiti on the walls only added to the creepiness.

Oakwood trees taller than the high walls stood for extra protection from the gangbangers. On the other side of the gate, was a small cylinder-like barrack big enough for a security guard to go for napping without people noticing.

The final line of defense was good old Jonathan for now. We bothered John in the middle of the night, jumbling up his sleep cycle. He walked up with pace, clicking tongues at every step.

"Cody?" John mouthed, putting on his reading glasses. He continued staring at the 18-wheeler and the drunk-as-hell Devon beside me with authority: an attempt at getting me to talk on the matter. It worked though. The way he looked at me like I kidnapped his daughter, I couldn't help but fill up the silence.

"We're... We're late after work. Devon Ledger, Jonathan. Jonathan, Devon Ledger." Introducing a guy drunk out of his mind to a confused guard who probably would never see the other ever after that night wasn't the best of choices. "You ask me what the hell am I doing driving a trailer truck at midnight? Well... that's quite a question you ask me, John-o. It's only the October Season if not anything else — when the workload is heavier than your belly — know what I mean?"

Right as I shut my mouth, I knew my nerves screwed me up — making me look creepier than ordinary. Why should he ever know the first word about the October Season or whatever when I myself had not heard of it until a second ago?

"Know what? ... Just-just open the gate, mate." I declared making it look like *he* was the one *I* was tired of.

First things first, coming from a mile away, you'd bet we reeked of low-grade whiskey. While I tried to talk ourselves in, my co-worker couldn't stop squirming in his pants. Devon stepped out of his seat, wanting to make a deal with John... Above everything, no person in his right mind would drive back home in a semi-truck without a reason good enough to back him.

All this while, John opened his mouth not for once. The chances of him checking the back of the truck shot up every second. It would have been the stupidest thing to get busted by a goddamn security guard. You bet your ass John would speak of it pretty proudly for the rest of his life. I pulled Devon inside. "Do not ruin this for me. You're high and he could tell for sure."

As Devon sobered up on one side, I got to talking with John, tipping him well above his day's salary. But I figured what the heck, it's an occasion after all. I ended up telling him that we were drunk by a few too many shots. He couldn't care less once his pockets grew a few bucks thicker. I drove the truck in.

• • •

"Cody, wait a second." Right when I said out loud that we'd made it, John called back. *Any transport unknown to the quarters should be thoroughly checked before being allowed inside*: it said in large font, right before my eyes on the information board. Under the printed text, was the official seal from the Residents' Association. Shit.

John marched towards my side of the vehicle. I could feel my heart beating. I chanted verses after so long. A voice inside me rambled: I told you so. Devon said it would only be fair to give ourselves up to the cops. My body heated up and ran cold at once. The incident, a few hours ago, seemed like a string of bad and very bad ideas.

John knocked on the door with his metal baton. "Guys... Cody, hear me out... I hate to do this to you." Devon turned his cheek the other way but I had nowhere to turn to. "You make sure you park the trailer *behind* the storage facility. And thanks for the money. You know how people stopped tippin' me these days? At least, there are good kids like you, of course... One day in the future, I'll be gone, and then, those misers will regret all of it..." He wouldn't leave me be, despite having no good topics to yap about. "Ah, what's the point?"

He shook my empty hand hanging out the window. "... So, then I'll see ya around."

As he walked back to his chair, my life came back to me. I'd never felt the taste of freedom more rewarding. We pushed into the building without looking back.

• • •

I parked the truck and turned the engine down.

"Damn, the residents' association put me out of life for one good second. Now, why should John remember the most important safety regulation when he's already busy enough with getting himself to fall asleep?"

Devon burst into the fakest of laughter to make me think he's quite cool about everything. To make me forget he wanted to surrender just about half a second ago. "Look at yourself. You would've been super-pissed had you been on the receiving end, is that not right? ... I can tell." He paused, the next second, to advise me on things he must be advising himself on. "Imagine what if he'd remembered the damn rule, if he'd checked the back. Dwell in the present, Cody... I tell you what, this better be the last time you tip this fatso."

All sounds died down. We figured it easier to sit in silence for some time. To catch up with thoughts that were far too difficult to put into words. I wiggled around, unable to keep calm. Having nowhere else to pointlessly stare at, I whipped out my watch: One to twelve. The sixteenth of October, 2007 was a rollercoaster ride haunting me to this moment.

John never considered confronting me. But we half-considered to end everything before helping myself to hear from him. With what was going on in the back of the truck, everyone seemed like a problem. Everything seemed so urgent. We'd soon go back to the way we were: that's what I hoped for, and it kept me running. Hell, how could I know then that no damn thing was getting any better? Not for once, no.

Devon heaved a sigh so tired, slowly opening his eyes to the bigger picture. He sifted through his pants rapidly before finding what he'd looked for. Two cigarettes. Why are there two of them, I thought.

"So, what seems to be the plan now?" He asked me.

No clue. My eyes ran dry. I wanted a break from running from anywhere and everywhere. Why are there two of them, I thought again. "You think, uh..." I put on a guilty voice, "... think you could spare me one of those cigarettes?"

I was a smoker my whole life. About seven years ago, I got a month-long job to take care of dying people in the local city hospital. When it meant absolution for my uncle, it meant a buck or two for me. I didn't really know then that taking care meant bathing and dressing up whiny old people with cancers and tumors.

Seeing a whole lot of half-dead people regretting the way they'd lived all their lives, I couldn't just get myself to smoke a pack without their last words looming over my head. I promised myself I would smoke no more cigarettes.

Devon, despite smoking a thousand cigarettes a day, always respected me for that, particularly because he knew he'd choose a good smoke over a long life. But I guess, only when you know you're *this* close to death, you don't give a damn about keeping promises.

Someone could break into my house and stab right at my chest for all I knew. I was only just done committing a bad, bad crime.

He got down the truck grabbing one of the two cigarettes without a word of wisdom. He was not up for advising me again and, hell, nor was I up for listening to one again. "Devon, you'll light this for me?" I only called for a lighter and he looked at me like I wasn't already sorry. I didn't ask for his life. But it was the first time he saw me smoke. The first time he saw me give in to smoking after fighting over it a hundred other times and holding myself strong every single time. But today was not a day for principles.

My seven-year streak broke off. I puffed the smoke in.

He smoked his and I smoked mine, alone and until the very last. A relief for the time being. At the cost of breaking the only promise I ever kept. It ate me up from the inside.

But today was not a day for principles. "There, next to the one with grills on the balcony." I showed him my one-bedroom apartment on the fourth floor of the five-story building. "We're sticking to the plan. Let's go up there if you're done."

"If by *plan*, you mean storing it here, are you positive you can store everything in your place only? I mean, looking around, it doesn't look very safe. And just so you know, my place is safer, and twice as big."

I didn't appreciate it when people spoke badly of my home. It was not the best but it was my first ever investment and I earned it. I am no Devon. I had no grandmas leaving behind their apartments for me.

"Devon, look at me. We both said yes to bringing the truck *here*. Sure, that was before I showed you around, but mine is one of the few houses here that has not ever been robbed. Not that I know of. I mean, what are the odds?" It sounded way better in my head. "They probably know I've got nothing." I laughed off my words.

He just couldn't acknowledge my humor. "Yeah, that's... sad. Let's say you're right. But since yours apparently has not been robbed at all, maybe yours is the next target. If I turn out to be right, what seems to be Plan B?"

I couldn't be nice all day. "There's no Plan B. This *is* the Plan. I'm not giving you a second option. You never trust me."

He put his palms in the air, finishing up his cigarette. "Okay, man. Whatever. Chill out."

We were so into moving the truck out of the spot, we never considered talking about what should be done once we made it. I couldn't help but suggest storing it all in my apartment and he had no better idea. We were first-timers. With no prior knowledge of the business, you can't blame me.

I'm not yet man enough to take up the blame for everything.

• • •

"Think no less of me. Now, welcome home." I said, pushing the door away. It flew open with a squeak. Across the doorway, I had set up a fish tank to make up for the smelly water pipes that leaked through the winter. A lonely goldfish swam inside. The walls were painted pistachio green when I moved in two years ago. The tiles were of black marble. If the colors don't seem to match up in your head, it doesn't need to. It never did and I didn't welcome enough people to consider repainting the walls or changing the tiles.

"So... How's the house?" I asked. I knew what he'd say. I knew what anyone would say.

"Would you make some coffee?" He took no notice of being asked a question. But I didn't say No.

To pair with the coffee, I lit myself another cigarette. One of the many I helped myself with, from Devon's collection. It didn't last fifteen seconds before I put it out on the kitchen wall... I couldn't live with half-smoking a tube of guilt every time before I go ahead and stub it out after a puff or two.

"Cody... I need you here." I heard Devon call me from inside.

What we had stashed away in the truck was huge. Above and beyond fantasies. We opened the closets, ripped out the drapes, undid the carpets, and pulled out the drawers. It didn't take so long to ransack my home. Not one place appeared safe enough to hide stuff. Only if I had given up and gone back to Devon's, we wouldn't have been wasting valuable time here. "Stupid-ass house" I heard Devon mumble once.

He was now done with everything but my ancestral wardrobe jammed to the wall. It couldn't have been of any good use at that point. But the way it sat on my floor, not letting anyone move it single-handedly teased his interest. "Give me a hand," he called. Again, I didn't say No.

We joined forces and moved it away from the wall far enough to sneak a look. The paint coated onto the wall hidden behind the wardrobe had broken down to particles. My pistachio green had faded so badly the wall looked half-white. Visible cracks ran through everywhere from inside, no doubt a few strong kicks were all it would have taken to break the wall down. With gangbangers zooming about the highway every now and then, this shouldn't be a good find.

"Jesus fuckin' Christ." Devon pulled me away, kicking me over and over until I turned away to save myself from a bleed. Kicks which the wall deserved.

He locked me by my collar. "Where's Plan B? Tell me, what the heck is Plan B now?" He screamed into my ears. His nails were pressing down by skin. I missed my chance to take him down a peg or two, right then and there. So, he didn't stop. "You think I'm out of my mind to let you hide my treasure in your crooked house? Heck, I'd leave em' on the streets but not in your place. What was that again — *trust*. You ask me why I never trust you with anything, there's your answer."

He was possessed by the devil. Being used to laughing at him getting angry, now it wasn't all that easy. It was the first time I'd seen him that way — the first time I'd seen his greed, rage, and whatnot... It, for sure, wasn't the last I saw him like that.

Tension filled the air. Ledger twisted around thoughtlessly. After a whack, a yell, and a deafening silence, he didn't know where to take it from there. Initially, I planned on feeling sorry for misleading us. But since he laid his hands on me, I had the upper hand. He pulled his hands to him, rubbing at my wrinkled collars. He couldn't unkink the wrinkle. I leaned backward, pushing him away from me, "Don't even try."

I'd had just about enough the other day. I didn't have, in me, the energy to fight back. In a few seconds of thinking, I got my words together. "Let's everybody be cool. Time's running out. I'll drive the truck out... Yeah, I'll drive the truck out of here." I helped myself to the time again. "Well, it's 1:30, good god. I'll get some sleep for Christ's sake." My voice cracked pathetically. "New plan: we leave by 5 and move the truck to your place, first thing in the morning."

I didn't wanna pretend like nothing happened. Following a needed pause, I picked up some balls. "I'm trying to forget it and move on. Get out of my sight for your good and get some sleep if you can. Whatever's the deal with you and me, tomorrow's a big day."

I made myself the bigger man after he beat me up. I found it the best possible way to handle everything then. Not as if I couldn't beat him up too. "... One more thing. You know I can kick you too."

I gave him the bedroom and settled for the couch. Not generosity, no. I've always found my couch more intimate. Like it could hold every confession I'd ever made behind its cover... And this time, there were more than a few confessions to make.

The lights faded.

From the TV cabinet, I pulled out the red colored shoebox. Leaning against the windowpane, making the most out of whatever light came through to my side, I scoured through its contents in the quietest way possible. I had to see for myself. I had to make sure that I'd not be the first man down when push came to shove.

Having confirmed my own safety, I hid the shoebox right where it belonged, and dropped to the couch before he could find me sneaking around.

CHAPTER II

Regression

October 17, 2007

A cold breeze swept through the half-opened windows ventilating the place. In the middle of the house, on the cramped couch, I tried going to sleep, flattening a pillow between my thighs. The recurring episodes of anxiety, the idea of choking my friend to death: it was one of the two doing the damage.

Near the living room was my bedroom, with a steel cot and a thinned-out mattress. It couldn't get too comfortable. But any man should have been well asleep by then, bearing in mind the day we had just fought through. I didn't move a muscle. Yet, I could bet Devon wasn't sleeping either.

"Cody..." shouted Devon, just like I had imagined. The coffee seemed to be doing its job of keeping me wide awake. "Cody, you awake? ... I couldn't fall asleep on your bed."

"I'm awake, all right. You're awake too but my bed has nothing to do with this. I sleep on it every day. I sleep just fine."

Devon stepped out of the room, wiping the sleep off his eyes. Relieved at his interruption, I finally stopped trying to go to sleep.

Without another word, he went for a hug to make up for what had happened already. Isn't a hug the easiest way out of anything, I thought, returning his hug anyway. "Now that we are awake, and have time to kill... what do you say we get the job done?" he asked.

"Do what? Care to explain yourself a little more?"

"Alright, my man, you *know* what I'm talking about. I asked you before, can't wait anymore." He talked all sugary right after kicking me in the ass: I couldn't get in on that one bit. "I wanna make sure we're on the same page with this."

"Alright." I said stiffly. "I know what you're talking about... Don't you think it's a little too late to uh..." I implied a question, peeping outwards and downwards through the ripped-apart curtains.

"No, not at all..." Quite frankly, I looked forward to it. We were finally getting to it.

• • •

We were dressed up at 3 in the morning. A lonely moon lit up the night sky. Silence gripped the air. In a weaker state of mind, I tucked three cigarettes in my pocket just in case. Both of us slipped into *regression* in just under one day of hitting the jackpot. Be it Devon acting up every other minute, be it me falling back into old ways. I knew I needed to stop smoking again. I did it once, why not again? Maybe not immediately, but I'll quit.

There we were, parading out the doors, caught up in the madness, while all else was indoors. Be it a gloomy night, or a sunny day, we had some errands to run by. Like John told me to, I had parked the truck behind the storage chamber.

The storage chamber had been locked for twelve whole years. All the way away from the apartment building — dirty, crammed with cobwebs, and possibly a haunted spirit — no one cared to open it up after all this time. I'd say, we got ourselves the safest spot there is.

I opened the double-doored cargo container. As the door spread out, darkness surrounded me. I had to make do with a single torch.

After swinging the torch here to there for a million times, eight three-foot tall cylindrical red boxes closed with nothing but a brittle lid showed themselves up in one frame.

I could picture the events that had led us there, without wanting to. I threw myself to the floorboard, my eyes fixed on the unopened boxes. "What do we do now? I feel so..." *Overwhelmed*. "... I don't know." Overwhelmed was the word I looked for. Even so, I smiled so shamelessly.

"Now, we do what should have been done already." Devon pulled a box to him. Heavy as it was, he could only ask me why it shouldn't be. He lifted the round black lid. We shot a look deep into the box, like children peeking down the water wells. Stacks and stacks of money so far as my eye could see. My bones trembled.

What we had in there was eight tubs of cash.

Not one, not two, but eight frickin' boxes full of dollar bills.

As soon as I set sight on the boxes, adrenaline rushed through to every corner of my body. It all happened so quickly. I had zero time to think about the problems that could come with it.

So far as I could recollect, all we had were a few seconds to get the money and the truck safe and away from the spot. We never cared to check if someone was spying on us. God forbid, what if it was all a trap?

Now that we had more than a matter of seconds in our hands, we couldn't sit around doing nothing. Before pounding our heads for every decision we ever came up with, we deserved more than a second-long glimpse. We deserved a day or two to only toy around with the money to so much understand the high-stake mishmash we got ourselves into. And that's exactly what we were about to do: Open every single one of them, cash crates.

One after the other, the lids were broken. Tubs after tubs, the cash, out in the open.

We fished out each one of those money to see how much floor it could cover. There isn't really a hell lot to do with money inside a locked truck. But we couldn't get ourselves to leave home as well. With a mountain full of George-Washingtons right by your shoulders, I couldn't possibly ask for something more. I wanted to sit there and do nothing.

"I'm starting to believe in miracles." I said. Less to appreciate the miracle that I said it to be, and more to shake down the sense of power growing inside of me and help myself realize it wasn't the end of the road yet.

It's no clever thinking to expect a guy who doesn't own a goddamn TV to not go bonkers all over when he sits over wealth that's worth over a hundred lifetimes of his.

"Stop right there a second." And there came the words of Devon Ledger to spoil every fantasy of mine in the blink of an eye. "I might be way out on a limb here, but..." I couldn't move for a second. He sounded like we had completely missed something. Like none of anything mattered now. A matter of seconds between his words seemed as long as a hundred lifetimes. "... Cody, is this real money? Are we sure that every bit of it is actual money?"

All that I ever dreamt of came crashing down now. Among the thousand questions I asked myself since the previous night, this wasn't one. Is this real money?

• • •

When I said to myself it couldn't get any harder, I did *not* mean a challenge.

I picked up a note, sizing it up from all four sides. I couldn't tell it apart from any other dollar bill I'd seen before. But, when had I ever practiced picking out fake bills from real ones? "We don't have any cash on us, do we?" I asked.

"Sorry, it didn't strike my mind to pick up my wallet. As I remember it to be, we were just about to open *eight fucking tubs of money*!"

I began running back to my place in search of a one-dollar bill. I could hear loud noises from inside the truck. Of Devon punching the metal body of the truck without a break. He was losing his shit again. Lots of Money and Angry Men: Never a lovely couple.

I returned with my wallet in moments.

He had just turned over a fresh tub with a grunt. A huge pile of cash slid out of the box, falling out onto the dirty floor, fighting each other within a space so tight. None of what I'd imagined could come true for all I knew, but the sight of all that money dropping down to my feet one above the other did not feel normal in any right way.

Ledger pulled open my wallet: a few different bills added up to some $36 — half of them worn and torn by the edges. Carrying little to no hope, he dropped down to get the job done.

I couldn't think of anything all that time.

Better yet, I couldn't think of anything that I was thinking all that time.

• • •

"Is it real? No — Was that a dream?" I wondered. He frisked my body up and down. I'd been lying there for a good time, I believe.

"Hey, you alright?" I was breaking out of sleep bit by bit. I tried standing up. My legs struggled to find balance. "You passed out or what?"

A mess of banknotes spread around the tight space: It couldn't have been so easy even for a person fresh and awake to walk around freely. "Haven't been sleeping well these days." No, it was no dream. Everything was as real as real could get. "Don't come telling me it's because of my mattress. It's not. I'm the problem." I blabbered until I was fully awake.

"Well, I'm done going through every pile of cash on the floor." There was as much money on the floor as there was, inside the other unopened boxes. "Cody, it unfortunately seems as though we did win the lottery." He whooped. "You and me, we're going places, don't forget. Screw all this!" He said, looking particularly at my empty wallet.

"Oh... Wow, that's great, man. Great. That's great."

"That's it? That's how much enthusiasm that's left in you?" He asked me in disbelief. I produced more *enthusiasm*. Only this time he didn't know I was faking it.

Devon cracked his ribs after what he thought was the last of our problems. "We made it. I made it." He claimed, so wrapped up in himself. I was far too buried in thoughts, mostly questionable ones, to notice or react to anything.

• • •

Devon's house was on the other end of the city — no less than an hour away. After an hour of stuffing all the dough back into the seemingly unfitting boxes, it got to quarter to seven in the morning. An orange sun lit up the morning sky. We'd fallen behind the schedule.

We shifted the truck and fled out of the entrance.

I had just won myself eight boxes of money. But I didn't jump around like Ledger. A lifeless bother from the inside; neither happy nor particularly sad. Was it because the money wasn't legit? No. It's not about legal and illegal. To me, I deserved it all.

But again, with all due respect, what good is a darned lottery ticket if you can't ever cash it out? Like any other time for the past 12 hours, I kept myself busy with the same old reason that there was work to do. Honestly speaking, an *excuse* is the right way to put it.

I got myself thinking about different things. We kept each other busy with cringe-worthy questions on how we'd live our lives after all of this.

Out of nowhere, a sound erupted from the base of the engine as if we bulldozed through Lego blocks. *Grggh*! The vehicle stopped in the middle of the expressway.

"We were low on fuel last night." Devon cursed.

"Hey, at least on the bright side, we're not on a busy road." I said. My words flew right through his ears like usual. The gas station was half a mile down the opposite side. And we had to walk all the way to buy fuel.

The truck decided to stop running right when we were having a hard time managing time as it was. But, was that a sign? A sign that we should have stopped and thought over things. A sign that we were not quite there to think about anything that had nothing to do with eight red tubs with cash in them. That at least one of us should have considered that every single one of the banknotes was a one-dollar bill.

• • •

We soon had the truck running again. Running through alternating landscapes of buildings and barren lands with houses and buildings getting more in number as we drove further and further into the city. Lumps of people moved all around everywhere. Living away from the city and the people wasn't a choice I made. It was the choice I had to make to make a living out of whatever I made. Now, I had quite a bit of money. So, do I finally get to move to the city?

When Devon asked me earlier where I wanted to live with all this money, I said I didn't know. Say what you will, I'd been a Clevelander for so long. I wouldn't be so cool if we had to move out of the city soon. Probably out of the state, we didn't know yet.

All this slowly got me thinking about the money again. With a bit of hesitation, I brought up a conversation I'd been wanting to for quite some time. "Devon. Tell me if I'm wrong. We're neck-deep into driving the truck round and round. But it doesn't end here, does it? I mean, we're messing around like everything is cool. But it isn't. I don't think we're careful enough. I just don't." The 'tell me if I'm wrong' meant nothing to me. I knew I wasn't wrong.

Devon pumped the brakes hard. I jerked forward, giving my head a small bump. "What now?" He was done with questions and doubts already but they weren't stopping anytime soon.

"Wait a second. You really think this is the end of the road? You hit the jackpot, good for you. But don't think all that's left is to get drunk and party all day."

"I never said that." He interrupted. I chose not to notice.

"... I say you're wrong this time. I feel-strike that. I *know*... we've not come face to face with the real deal yet. This is not the time to think about what you'll do when you get there when you don't know if you'll get there at all. We'll soon run into open ends. Open ends where money alone is not gonna cut it." It didn't look like he was taking me seriously. "Because you were wrong about the *fake money, real money* drama doesn't mean doubt is bad. Doubt is good, especially when you don't know shit about what you're gonna be doing a day from now. Do you not hear me, man?"

"Jesus, stop crying like a baby for a second, all right? We have money that the people around us can only dream about. But you're acting like all this is some goddamn punishment. Yeah yeah. I thought so. You're just not cool enough." He said all this so quickly like he'd been dealing with money since he could remember.

"Shut up." I banged the seat like it was his head full of pride. "Tell me you're nuts. But think for a moment before you call me names. I'll shoot a couple of questions off the top of my head. And if you have an answer for one — just one question — then I'll sign on a paper that says I cry like a fucking baby. Now, is that a deal?"

He pulled out the keys from the ignition and swung over to my side. "Fine. It's a deal."

"For starters, if you're looking to spend the money on buying something big for yourself, your hands are tied so long as this is illegal cash. How do you plan on making it all clean? You know very well you can't go around carrying a tub of money over your head." I let out a meaningful pass before pushing forward.

"Even, say you did so, what do you think people would think when they wake up one day and bam, you're rich! You're rich and you work at a company that's about to go broke." I could say he started taking me seriously. "I have no idea why anyone would be so damn nuts to leave eight, remember, eight whole tubs of money on the loose inside a garage that has no video cameras around. And I most definitely have no idea why you and I would be so damn nuts to actually take that money and run away.

"With so many questions and no answer, how do we stay safe from the police? After all, you're the guy who wanted to surrender fearing a fat security manager."

"That's different," screamed Ledger.

"Lastly, we have a family. Last I checked, both of us have families living out here in Cleveland. What's it gonna take to get them on our side? This lifetime? And that's enough, you think? There are more, but we'll stop for now, cool guy."

Like I thought, he couldn't say one damn word. I guess I gave it my all. His eyes popped out of his face but his mouth didn't consider opening up one bit. It was a little too late for him to understand things. But better late than never.

A huge container truck thrice the size of ours honked for its way. Devon came back to reality. He quickly turned the engine on, cornering our vehicle across the road. "Cody, I have nothing..."

He said, still holding on to the same tone. But he didn't say sorry. Nothing close to it. "My bad. I'll tell you what. Drinks on me tonight. Worst comes to worst, we can at least buy alcohol with that money, am I wrong?" He said with a laugh. Out of options, I nodded along.

A lot of questions in mind, but not quite as many answers. Thanks to me, the drive was only full of silence from thereon. We didn't dare to talk about how we could grow old in a 30-yard swimming pool, no. A part of me badly wanted this money. Another significant part of me regretted everything that had been happening for the last 15 hours and hoped I never caught sight of those eight sinister boxes.

• • •

The clock struck eight. It was only the second time I visited Devon's house. A hallway so narrow only one could walk at a time led to the squarish living room. The living room led into two other bedrooms and a kitchen but there just weren't as many things as the empty spaces that surrounded the house from all directions.

The walls were so white and stainless that the house held no life. An unfitting wall clock hung aloft. The couch, the chairs, and the cardboard boxes not been fully unpacked for half a year occupied insignificant places on a floor that seemed to come to an end nowhere. My place could hold the true meaning of the word dirty in all respects and it still seemed way more welcoming than this piece of concrete packed in nothingness and yet managing to suffocate me.

It was probably an overreaction. But when the last thing I could remember was Devon hating my place so much for so little reason, all I could come up with was everything that was wrong with the huge house of his. But it only lasted until he turned me around.

The hallway might have been narrow. But all that space it could have used up didn't go to waste. Beneath all the piled-up cardboard boxes, I saw a door facing the other way. The stairs went down and down until it was dark enough for people to hide things. Maybe, things as valuable as tubs of money.

"I like to block this doorway with these cardboard boxes so it looks like I have something stashed away in the basement." Devon spoke, slowly walking down the stairway. "Funnily enough, when I first moved in, I almost believed I did. That my grandmother left me something huge before she passed." Huger than this house?: I wanted to ask. "You know, like wills, or crazy wealth from long-lost relatives. I built all my hopes up only to see this." The tube lights lit up the dark room.

Potteries and half-done artworks were stacked up along the side walls. He didn't look very happy as he stared at everything his dying granny left behind. He felt cheated as if he did not get something he believed he should have gotten. All he got in return was a huge house. A huge house without enough things to fill it up with.

"The meeting is when? Half past eleven, right? Not a lot of time in hands." He said quickly. He was probably trying to fool himself too, with the same old reason that there's work to do.

We got to moving the boxes one after the other through the hallway and down the stairway. Before I could go ahead and tell him, it struck Devon how empty and suspicious the entire house seemed. He decided to bring all the age-old potteries and paintings to the living room, fouling up his tidy residence. Now we had with us eight tubs of money and two disordered households. We put the cardboard boxes back where they belonged and padlocked the basement door.

I hired a taxi at quarter past ten, tipping him dollars above the fare to break his fastest record in a Wednesday traffic. Also, to take us there in one piece.

The doors and windows were locked. We walked out with a tinge of fear that the empty house was now worth a whole lot more. We were about to work hard late nights for the next few days after which we'd part ways splitting the worth.

But the question of the hour - "How and Where did we come to find eight boxes full of money worth hundreds of thousands of dollars?" It all started four months ago...

CHAPTER III

A Retrospect

June 7, 2007

It all started four months ago.

The AC couldn't function all that well with 17 of us packed into a 15x10 room. But it was the only space with air-conditioning. Fourteen employees and three of the bosses occupied the small conference room. Jerome Biscuit sat comfortably at the round table facing us, with Jeff Walker and Daniel Jenson, two of his uplines. We were left standing for close to an hour now without a coffee break.

"It's not very simple after all," answered Jerome Biscuit to his boss sipping on his coffee. "If any of these men here are inefficient or a little too much to pay a fixed monthly salary, we can always cut back in salary or fire a few of them." Jerome Biscuit was our tall gray-headed boss: a nutcase known mostly for his sudden outbursts of anger and zero mercy for the people working under him. He knew just enough how much work can take all the fun out of an office job yet not be so sickening that you wanna kill yourself.

"Isn't that more or less what we tried to work with in Dayton, last winter? It didn't seem to work out very well," said Jeff Walker. It worked out well for at least himself, if not anyone else. After closing down the Dayton branch and chasing away all the employees, Daniel Jenson had no choice but to make Jeff the regional manager: a post made up right then and there just so that Jeff could still work for Jenson.

With bases spread around Cincinnati, Dayton, and Cleveland, Daniel Jenson was the C.E.O. of this crumbling architectural firm. Jerome Biscuit was only in charge of the employees in Cleveland. Jeff Walker was right next to Daniel Jenson on the ladder — now that he was bumped up to regional manager, whatever that meant.

"This is not Dayton, Jeff. Things could maybe change here for good," he replied, without putting an effort to hide how he wished he was in Jeff's shoes. He couldn't care less for what happens to the Clevelanders. And all this war of words was nothing but a stunt at getting Jenson's attention.

"Look, everybody, whatever decision we make today, it will only be for the good of *J.J.Designers*," said Daniel Jenson almost cinematically.

J.J. Designers was the only company to give me a job. I was either lucky enough to get interviewed by Daniel Jenson himself, or the company was so out of work for the CEO to go around interviewing people. By the words of Jerome Biscuit, my boss's boss was an even bigger sociopath.

"But, we need to ask ourselves this question: Do we really need to shut down another branch?" asked Jerome.

The months of June and July were the busiest for the accounting department. New projects were signed and their finances were taken care of. But, this year, it was a clean sheet for Cleveland. Not one new project was signed.

People had nothing to do. Some of us started selling the computers off record. There were nearly not as many people as computers and definitely not as much work to do as well. We couldn't afford to repair the security cameras. We were eventually gonna take them all away, including the one or two that actually worked. Garages full of loader trucks and heavy-duty machinery had been locked down for months. Even Jerome began to run out of things with which he could keep the fourteen of us busy.

Everyone in that room knew we had to shut down sometime soon enough. Following a couple of monotonous arguments between the three bossmen, they decided to break for lunch.

• • •

Devon Ledger sat with me at the cafeteria like usual. We worked in different parts of the company, but he always came back to me to keep himself entertained. We talked about how Jerome's marriage was falling apart, how Jenson had a drinking problem, and just about everything that had anything to do with the doomed company.

"Food and a roof over my head. That's all I have. Everything I spend my money on. I take the subway to the office every day and I've still not got money to buy some beer when I fucking feel like it. What, they could fire a few of us, as simple as that, isn't that right? Well, guess what? You'll see me quitting this week. What do you say?" Devon asked me.

My phone vibrated in my pants before it went off the next ring. There was a rule that said no phones should ring in meetings. There was also a rule that said no one should speak on the phone when Jerome was speaking: a few too many rules for a firm that couldn't pay its own people. "One bad meeting, Devon. Don't rush it for one bad meeting. Because, for one thing..." 7 missed calls. I stopped short. 7 missed calls from Michael Mills. *Cody, call back*: the message read.

"What's wrong?"

I pushed the chair aside, getting out of my seat as fast as I could. "Devon, I gotta go take this call." Michael Mills was not a man to make 7 calls to a person. If he was, he'd have called me back home that same night I ran away. I rushed to the balcony, away from the people and their noise. The phone rang again. But this time, from a different number.

Before cutting the call on impulse, I asked myself if it was him trying to reach me from a different phone. "Hello, who is it?"

"Good morning sir, we're calling from Richard Medical Centre. Is this Cody Mills I'm talking to?" answered a lady in a faint voice.

It'd been two years since I last talked to my uncle. He sat me down and asked me as softly as he could: "Look, Cody, you really think you're satisfied with your job?" I was making so little money he sometimes had to drive me to the office. I didn't complain, but he did. Reasonably so. But it rubbed me up the wrong way. I went in looking to win an argument. Possibly looking to convince him I was a burden. And I did. It was the last of our arguments and two years down the road, not much improved for me on the money end of things.

"Yes. This is Cody Mills, yeah." I remembered to answer.

"This call is about one Mr.Michael Mills. I take it you're his emergency contact?"

"Yeah." I didn't know I was still his emergency contact. But I couldn't come out just yet. "He's my uncle, alright. What the hell happened?"

"He's okay. He's resting." She said, taking it further. "About an hour ago, Mr.Mills walked into our hospital already looking pale. Before anyone could attend to him, he lost control and fell on his face. He's regained consciousness and is in good hands now, so there's no need to panic. You can come and visit him now. We're calling from Richard Medical Centre, Sixth Avenue, East Cleveland."

An artificial charisma underlined her words. One could only imagine she was reading it out from a paper. The one feeling I could easily sympathize with was job dissatisfaction.

"I'll be there." I hung up. The lunch bell was about to go off. I was left with choosing between going the right way and going the easy way. The right way meant to put myself through Jerome Biscuit and get his approval.

"You're letting me down like always." I heard him shouting in the bullpen before I turned away to take the stairs. I wouldn't wanna wait forever for him to calm down and understand where I come from. I paced myself to rush through the stairs before he called me over: "Hey, you got a minute?" It was Jeff Walker waiting for his elevator.

"Yes, sir." I said, before regretting why I didn't run away like I heard nothing.

"If down is where you're about to go, join me in the elevator for a conversation."

"Uh, yes, sir." I said, holding myself back in a little fear. It was the first time I was talking face-to-face to the new regional manager. I had no reason why he'd be interested in me.

"You can call me Jeff," he said sweetly. Almost too sweetly. "How do you like your office?" He asked then in a firmer tone.

"Can't complain." I was on my toes for the elevator door.

"Are you sure about that?" He waited to get the reply he wanted to get. Jeff was known to be a very private person. Known to avoid people unless it was important. The Dayton employees were always happier. They didn't have a superior dancing around them every minute.

"I mean, there are good times and bad... Things should get better." The door opened. Why did Jeff want to talk to an employee about the company? Not very bosslike. I kept my replies sharp without any leeway to build questions upon them. All I should be thinking about was getting to the hospital. Nothing else, for my own good.

"J.J.Designers is at its possible worst." Jeff read from a square piece of paper. "The revenues aren't coming through like they used to. The projects aren't getting signed like usual. Cincinnati is now the only city with a possible source of income. I think it is best that we close down on the Cleveland branch, cut short on manpower, and stay close to our home ground."

I had to mindlessly shift topics to take my leave. "Sir. Uh, Jeff, I really have to go now." I said as the elevator doors opened up on the ground.

"One moment." He handed the square paper to me. As I was deciding if I should go on and take it from him, he stuffed it into my shirt pocket. "Once we resume our meeting, I'll go for asking the employees' opinions. You are raising your hand before everybody else, and you are speaking what I've written down here without making it look like a rehearsed speech." He said without giving me the option to say anything otherwise. "Remember that you're doing yourself and the company a big favor." He said, again sweetly and turned around with a broad smile.

• • •

I was chosen to bat for Jeff Walker and his decisions at the afternoon meeting. But here I was, paying off my taxi ride at Richard Medical Centre. He was in no mood to ask me why I was going where I was going. Or if I could at least make it to the meeting. Getting off the building and on the taxi seemed to be the right choice.

A heavy odor of medical wastes brushed through the air already so chemically scented from the paint cartons arranged along the emergency exit. I signed the visitors' record. I was now some three doors away from my uncle in the general ward. The last conversation of mine with Michael Mills was an unpleasant one all the way back twenty-two months ago. But that unluckily wasn't the last time we were in the same room.

Waking up from a late night party, fatally hungover from being stoned crazy a few hours before, I ran into him at the worst possible time at a drugstore. I couldn't begin to imagine what mental image he would have formed of me when I probably looked like I hadn't taken a shower for a few days. Like I had lost my job and had been living on the streets. I chased myself out of the place, without paying the bill. The guard might have chased me for a distance but I was running away so fast I didn't find time to particularly run away from the aftermath. That was a year before. I'd successfully managed to keep myself off the other side of Cleveland since then.

"You can find Mr.Mills on the fourth bed to your right." I heard. Caught up in my head, I had walked all the way to the general ward. I pulled myself away from the doorknob.

"What do I say to him now?" I almost asked the nurse by my side. "Give me a minute to get my shit together." I told her before finding a better way to phrase my thoughts. "How about you leave me alone for a moment? I don't want him to see me when I'm already sweaty and my heart's racing... I mean, it might *alarm* him, am I wrong?"

The nurse walked away with a little nod. She understood me the way she wanted to. I didn't want it to look like I had come running over since I heard he was in the hospital. I didn't want it to look like

I cared for him when he already thought I was poor and desperate for money. That couldn't help matters. I escaped to an empty men's room for a little pep talk.

I stared at the mirror the way I wanted to look at him. I imagined myself walking up to him so slowly as though I don't really give a damn except he's family. Like I already have enough things to keep me busy. Maybe, also happy. "Hey there, Michael Mills. How's life treating you?" I practiced, with a trained sense of pride that I made it out alive.

But if I happen to succeed in making the old man lying deadbeat in the patient's bed pity me, if I let him go on and make conclusions only to offer me money out of his pocket, there would be no doubt on anyone's part that I'd be the biggest fucking failure: I thought.

• • •

His eyeballs moved around as he sensed movement by his bed. I stopped for a second, hoping he wouldn't notice and I could just disappear. In some way, it was all because of me. I did this to him. I abandoned him in the name of saving face. In the name of helping him ease off the burden that I was to him. While all I managed to do was rid myself of good company and rid him of a person to care for.

He opened his eyes and looked up. A stare of surprise or disbelief, maybe. He should have assumed I wouldn't have come. Or that I would have died on the road already of hunger.

He lay on his back, face all covered in warts and dark circles, his eyes — tired and sleep-deprived. A receding hairline with more gray than black hair scattered around a head half bald. Thinner than I remembered to be were his wrists and beard. His cheeks were more wrinkled, eyes more blackened. On any other day on a random roadway, a second-long look wouldn't have been good for me to recognize my uncle. He was not one bit of the man I knew him to be.

"Cody?" he asked doubtfully. He threw me out of my element. I forgot what I prepared for myself in the bathroom mirror. My mind blanked out on me.

"Hey..." I stopped. Do I call him uncle or do I call him Mike: I wondered, before deciding to leave the sentence hanging the way it was. "... How are you holding up?"

Mike pulled himself up, pressing his palm down the bed. He twisted in pain. My cheek turned the other way. I couldn't even hear him cry in pain without wanting to kick myself in the nuts. "I'm holding up just fantastic." He said, his voice full of a painful sense of irony. I wanted to say I was sorry. But if I really was sorry, I wouldn't have been to the bathroom to write myself an elaborate speech without a single word called sorry in it.

"The doctor told me you shouldn't strain yourself."

"The doctor tells you all kinds of nonsense, son." His hands toyed with all the medicines and bottles arranged on the table, pushing a couple of them to the floor. He pulled out an old set of keys from under the newspapers. His wrists shivered visibly. Keys that looked so familiar, fans that creaked so badly, foods that smelled so chemical, and beds that reeked of shit: I put my mind to everything around me except for the mess that he had made of himself.

He threw his keys to me. "Do you remember what this is?" He asked, getting his things together in a hurry. "Keys to my Chrysler." He paused and said so with a smile. The keys to his minivan — the minivan that took me to the office more than a decent number of times.

Small talks before the bathroom mirror couldn't stop me from smiling back at the good old days. "The Red Thunderbolt."

"Actually... the Black Thunderbolt. I had it repainted..." Tiny little smiles tried their best to make him look happier. But he had given up on happiness. I could tell. But I went where the moment took me. "How fast do you remember it could go back in the day? Some forty-fifty? Now we're just cruising through at thirty miles an hour." He exhaled with a disappearing smile. Tired of living some life in the last two years. *Some life.*

"Looks like the IV's getting done, should I call a nurse?"

"Not before you ask me why I called you so many times." He packed his bag with everything he got together and threw it to the other side of the bed like a man with a plan. "I called you because I didn't want you here."

"And... why is that?"

"But you're here after all... You have my backpack and the keys to the minivan. It is parked two buildings away. Black Chrysler, don't you forget. Meet me with the car out front in about five minutes." He tore the taped injection tube right off his wrist.

"For Christ's sake, I don't think you're supposed to tear it off. Uncle, you're sick. I'm not taking you anywhere." I yelled. "Why are you suddenly acting up like you're gonna rob the hospital?" He continued getting himself ready to leave the quarters.

"Quite the opposite. I'm trying to stop the hospital from robbing me." He stood up only for me to remember how terrible he looked. His legs seemed thinner than I had thought of. He didn't look like he belonged anywhere but a hospital bed. "Whether you like it or not, I'm walking out of here. It's up to you to decide if you're really gonna let your old man drive the car."

"I'm not playing by your rules, Mike. Do you all just assume that I can be bent in every way to get things done? Look at yourself. No, really... look at yourself."

He tried to play me the exact same way Jeff Walker did, that very afternoon. It killed me to come to understand how everybody looked at me the same way. Including my uncle who wasn't even fit enough to stand upright and not look like a humanoid robot.

"Listen to me Cody, I can only tell you this. If you wanna hear more of it, then help me out here." He said, choosing his words carefully. "Cody, I..." He hesitated. "I might have got the cancer."

• • •

With the black Chrysler blocking the way to the entrance out front, I signaled over to my uncle heading out with a bag slung over his shoulders. When a practically empty bag already discomforted his hands, I couldn't begin to see how he'd have driven the minivan up to the hospital in the first place. To say *cancer* and hesitating to explain further was just his way of pissing people off.

"Let's go," he said, very proud of himself as he managed to take his seat near me.

"Tell me what's going on. And then we'll go." Moving cars began to honk at us as they passed. The hospital guards began to give us the eye as they passed. I asked him the same question twice, thrice, and again. "Fill me in. Fill me in and then we'll go."

"Cody, please, we'll talk somewhere private. Let's go to our place."

"I'm not coming to your place. I told you I won't come again. Nothing has changed since." I said, only with the intention of pulling something out of him at the earliest.

"Well, where the hell do you wanna go at three in the afternoon? A fricking bar?"

• • •

The Homelanders: a faded neon sign under the afternoon sun helped us identify. We found the nearest bar six blocks away. At this odd hour, only the most dedicated of daily drinkers were sitting at each of the corners of the squarish tavern. It was neither the busiest day nor the busiest hour: the perfect place for people to have long-winded discussions so long as you don't care for the turned-down air conditioners for apparently commercial reasons. It was hotter than outside, but I couldn't wait long enough to find a better place.

I went for a table least accessible by the bartenders, hoping no one would come by asking for my usual. "So, you've known this for five months now, you're losing hair faster than before, you have no clue what's going on inside your body, and you think it's best to run away from a hospital, tearing off the injection tube."

"Cody, sit down and we'll talk." After avoiding him for two good years, I had no business knowing how bad the cancer was. But he thought I did and I couldn't get myself to give up on that edge. I was never getting a chance to boss someone and that one conversation reminded me to massage my ego every now and then. I'm not proud of myself. But for being the lap dog in every other conversation, it was my one chance to blow off steam.

"Get a doctor, you know that's the right thing to do." He shuffled in his seat, looking behind me. He badly needed his usual whiskey and he didn't make a move for it. If I would have signed off on that or not is another, but, to me, it could only mean one thing. "Are you short on money?" He was bringing himself to laugh it off. "You're short on money, aren't you?" This time, I was right on the money.

"Cody, money is never a problem. Look, I... uh, I'm seventy-two, do you understand what it means to be seventy-two? Life isn't as colorful anymore, that's the truth. And, I..." He stopped and looked away. "... I think I need a drink." It was my business to offer him to buy one. But I wanted him to come out with the truth on his own, preferably without putting my wallet to use. There was an off chance for me to have been poorer... At least, I hadn't gotten cancer.

"I lost my job. I've lived enough, Cody."

"I'm not seventy-two, but I know seventy-two is not long enough. I think you should stop looking for whiskey and go get a doctor." We took the next minute to ourselves, with both of us in some position to come up with a better solution. For all the demands and questions I helped myself with, I had to step up. "Do you need money?" I began, knowing he would remain silent forever, if otherwise. His self-worth was in the shade for the first time.

"Oh, Cody, no. I don't want to put you in that place." He still said. "This is exactly why I didn't want you here. I've lived my life, and I honestly cannot do this to you. You've got a life ahead of you, I'll take care of myself." When he said he didn't need me, I assumed he needed me the most. "I don't need your help, soon."

"How much would it cost, a few thousand dollars?"

"That wouldn't do more than just finding out what went wrong." He declared, now a little more forwardly.

"Then, let's find that out first. I'll get the cash ready, I'm on good pay now." I lied through my teeth casually. I believe I was good though. He actually believed I was on good pay. Now he didn't attempt to refuse my money. All he needed to accept the help graciously was for me to insist twice like I was the one benefitting from it. It's only human to be that way. I bet he began thanking his God right that moment.

I decided to leave him alone before he could come up with more questions to follow up. "You don't want me driving you home, do you? Will you be okay by yourself?" I asked for the sake of asking, with no idea how to get my hands on some few thousand dollars. I was fucked. He nodded slowly.

CHAPTER IV

Something Unforgivable

June 7, 2007

Jerome was always the last man out of the office. But 10 p.m. is a little too late even for him. As if something stopped him from leaving early. The city grew quieter with the passing hour. My heart almost gave up waiting for him. I should have walked off right then and there. I would have, if not for Devon holding me back. He convinced me this was what I wanted.

J.J.Designers had been leasing out the underused parking lot to the textile clusters around the area. We knew there should be enough cars for us to hide beneath. After an hour or two of staying put with half a heart, Jerome Biscuit walked to his car parked all the way across the maintenance wing.

I had been hearing leaves rustling behind the thorny shrubs. But Devon didn't. We were just done putting on the robber masks. I could swear someone was watching us go. I felt the rush in me: feeling fully alive after so long.

"You know what these are called?" asked Devon, proceeding to answer without giving me time to think. "*Balaclavas*."

Long rows of vehicles — big and small — faced each other on either side of the alleyway. We had to keep our guards up for the next half a mile, making sure to give away a headstart good enough for him to not notice two of his employees wanting to go at his money. I pulled down my balaclava time and again to ensure there was no way he could recognize me. The alleyway grew darker and darker. After a point, we could hear no sound but the running machinery of the textile mills. Right by the plan.

The entry gates were locked shut. Hoping to God no one else would care to stroll through the parking lot at 11 in the night, we got our hand-knives in order. We had put in motion the worst of plans. Devon and I were just about to knock down Jerome Biscuit to the ground. We were gonna rip off our own boss to pay our bills.

I wasn't even mad at Jerome anymore. We were making a mistake. "Devon, do we really have to do this?" I asked, in a whisper.

He was far enough for him to dodge the question making it look like I wasn't loud enough. I knew I shouldn't be any louder. He continued tailing Biscuit as he carried his satisfied self to his car. Devon didn't hear me begging him to pull the brakes. Decidedly so.

• • •

I made it to the bullpen as voices overlapped one another from a room filled with confused minds. Some of them left the office, some rushing in and out of the conference room, some screaming at others, and some getting screamed at by others.

It felt fair to go back to the office before anything. It was only sensible to meet with Jerome and tell him why I couldn't make it to the rest of the meeting. Only a few hours from what looked like an unending war, everybody was already found running from one end to the other. It seemed as if they had already come to an agreement and I wasn't a part of it. I couldn't find Devon anywhere in the mix.

Between an army of men and women fighting for documents and computers, a set of eyes observed every movement of mine. He didn't care to look away well after I spotted him sizing me up. He meant for me to see him there in the cafeteria, with a cup of coffee in one hand, and a notepad in the other: its papers, the same color as the one conveniently folded up in my chest pocket. I had comfortably forgotten to deal with Jeff Walker.

Jerome Biscuit seemed easier to deal with. I rushed into his cabin, pushing aside the associates. "Evening, Mr.Biscuit." I walked into him as he hung up on someone on the other side.

He glanced at me up and down, shrinking his reddish face. "What part of *Don't come to me without an answer* did you not understand?"

"What, no, but..." He walked back to his chair, his round little face giving me a wrinkled eyebrow stare that I still remember to hate. I could only assume he couldn't tell me apart. "I'm-I think you've misunderstood me. See, I had an emergency. A family one."

"Who the hell are you?"

"I'm Cody Mills, I work for you."

"What's your problem then?" He interrupted, almost setting me off.

"Sir, hear me out. I couldn't come to the afternoon meeting. My uncle ended up in the hospital." I answered quickly, yet consciously.

"You didn't come to the afternoon meeting? You didn't come to the meeting and you walk into my office and go: *Evening, Mr.Biscuit.* Boy, you have no idea how badly I wanna fire your ass."

"Sir, I just told you about my uncle, I didn't want to go away..." I lost track of what I should have said and what I ended up saying. Hearing him say *fire* only sometime after I heroically raised to the occasion, all I could think about was my stupid promise. I wasn't already doing very well financially.

"Why are you telling me all this? I don't give a shit about your uncle. I'm just done assuring Daniel that we're gonna do twice as much as yesterday. You'd already be on your way home if not for that."

"Just tell me what I should do."

Biscuit filled up his briefcase, beginning to clear the room. "Go out there and ask questions. Don't come wagging behind me for every single thing like a stupid fuck." I had not ever seen him swear at an associate before. I'd have much preferred it was someone else than me for his first time. I still decided to stay mute and deaf. I had very little time to earn so much money. "We have one goal and one goal only in mind. Let your uncle rot in hell for all we care," he said, walking past me.

"That is unnecessary." I said to his back. "You shouldn't have said that..." I replied, right as he abandoned me in his room. " ... you stupid fuck." There was no way he could have heard me in all that chaos. I had no reason to hesitate. "Stupid fuck, that's you." I kicked his table a couple of times, before finding my way back.

• • •

I didn't know if he had any money stashed in his car. We only made the move since he should be having upwards of a thousand dollars on him. We were sure of it. The bosses only got together on paydays. Jerome just seemed like the type of guy who'd prefer to move around with some cash in hand rather than a bank account. Of course, we knew we could be wrong.

We reached the end of his trail. There were no more cars to slouch under. Jerome was a few yards away, seconds from driving off. I had no idea if Jerome possibly knew it all along. He reached into his pockets for his keys. The headlights beeped on from a distance. Devon looked at me, almost hesitant to make a move: one last moment of self-doubt. Whatever the situation, it was either now or never.

I led the way, being careful not to call him out at any point in time. If at all my voice struck a chord in his memory, it would at least cross his mind that it was the same guy he made a joke out of, that same evening. To do it the right way, we had to stay quiet the entire time. I had to ask him to hand over his wallet without asking him. Or better yet, I had to push him down and grab at his butt all while making it clear I was only there for his money. Devon kicked down a few buckets that were arranged one atop the other. Jerome turned back in surprise. It was *go time.*

• • •

I sat next to Devon with a cold lunch at five in the evening. "Will you tell me now what your problem is? You're being a five-year-old," he said.

"My uncle's sick. He's gonna die if I don't take him to a doctor. He's gonna die anyway, well at least this way, we'll know what's coming when." He nodded, with a couple of reactions here and there: not too careless for me to quit going further, yet not too comforting for me to feel weird about it. My uncle's dying, it's not the end of the world. I continued. “I need some $5000. And yeah, I’m walking a fine line between poor and broke.”

“I’m not the person to advise you on this, you know that. What I *can* tell you is that I don’t have a damn clue how you’ll earn five grand the right way.”

“What do you mean *the right way*?”

“You know what I mean. So, what are you saying, is this how you’re gonna make it right with Biscuit for shitting on you?”

“What the heck are you talking about? What’s he got to do with this?”

“Well, I mean, you’re angry and you’re going crazy, telling me how he crossed his lines and how you’re not gonna spare that son of a bitch. Five minutes later, you’re telling me this. Look, I’m not giving you any ideas.” He said, giving me an idea. Devon’s always got his way with me where he convinces me that he’s helping me when all he’s doing a favor for is himself. In fact, everyone does.

“That’s crazy. Are you actually suggesting... No, that’s too crazy.” I began filling the air with words as I wrapped my head around this newfound idea. He let me have the moment and process it all before he interrupted me.

“This is your uncle we’re talking about. Jerome’s not a great guy, is he?” He asked me, hitting the right notes. I shook my head hesitatingly. I wanted to hear more. “I can’t give you money because we’re in the same boat. But I can help you see the truth. Taking what’s not yours isn’t right, but what he did to you isn’t right too.”

“No, forget it. I’ll figure something else out. I’ll take out a loan.” I owned no property for collateral. Moneylenders look for that. I could never get a bank to trust me that I’ll repay them, because, for one thing, I can’t.

“Alright, you don’t have to say anything.” I stopped him before he could go ahead and stress the obvious. “How do I do this all by myself?” He shrugged, meaning to say he was interested without saying so. I had to make it clear, out and loud, that I was only agreeing to what was his own master plan. “Wait a second, just so we’re entirely sure, are you asking me if we can somehow rip off our boss?"

• • •

I pushed my hand away to a brighter region, showing off my knife in a frenzy. He put his hands in the air, taken by surprise and fear. Devon joined me, closing down on Jerome from all sides. "Who are you? Please. What do you want?" I could only hear him asking all of these time and again for a whole minute. He breathed heavily, clouding most of what he said in those moments.

We cornered him against the brick wall, his keys thrown about on the ground. Since we couldn't exactly talk, neither of us could understand each other. He took some time to himself before he understood it wasn't just a bad dream. He slowly slid onto the ground, babbling how he was harmless. We stood there, with a finger on our lips, shutting him up by all possible means. I couldn't concentrate.

I looked around for a moment. I could feel all eyes on me, but thankfully not. We were masked up too, I remembered. Not even double-layered linen could save me from feeling naked from within. I noticed Devon hunting the guy's coat pocket for wallet, money, and all sorts of valuables. Out of what leaked out, it was visiting cards outnumbering coins and dollars, a perfume bottle, a pack of smokes, and a pocketbook. We didn't quite hit the jackpot with what he had on him. Devon showed me off to the next stop.

I made my way to his car. Sounds were getting louder than before. My partner couldn't do a damn thing without saying a thing or two. He flinched back and forth for a second, stuck between decisions. My boss began to hold the situation until I realized this was my one chance. "Lookit, this is not gonna..." Right in the stomach, I kicked him hard.

He jerked for a second, a yelp from inside shutting off all other noises he made. He crawled to the other side, guarding his stomach. His pantsuit was muddied. I paused for a moment to see if I was walking myself into a life I wouldn't appreciate. I didn't live my days to beat up people I had a problem with. It did not feel like a normal day. Of course, it wasn't. But no amount of self-talk could save me from kicking the hands guarding his body.

Devon Ledger, of all people, was stunned at me for making a move he couldn't himself make. I wasn't playing his game anymore. He walked to the car as I showed him off, picking up the keys. Jerome glanced out of the corner of his eyes, remembering to pay one part of his attention to my shoe. If I were to go any further, I had to go all the way in. There should be all the time in the world to regret that night. I wasn't stopping halfway anyway.

"Where's your money?" I asked, without thinking. I gave myself away.

• • •

I preferred staying overtime. There was no guarantee I would ever come back had I gone back home. Only for all the courage I built over time to collapse alongside me.

At sunset, we set up camp in the parking lot. Ledger got his hands on two sharp knives apparently from a pawn shop around town. He asked me if we could use a gun. We could, except, with a gun, you never know what goes wrong. Knives are no-nonsense. On a side note, we weren't there yet. It's the only reason, probably. "A gun? You gotta be kidding me. What, are we working for the mafia now?" It was anybody's appropriate reaction.

We go back if Jerome walks out earlier than usual, we go back if there are more than three people around at the time. We go back if one of us wants to. These were the conditions I said yes to. All in all, we roll out if everything, down to the last detail, favors the hold-up. Things never go right for me, and it was some confidence in me that said we'll get to leave before anything happens. Things had to go wrong for good.

Day workers pulled out their cars as night-shifters settled in. It's around 8:00 when Biscuit calls it a day. Footfall fell in number as we waited in the distance for Jerome Biscuit. Save for a few millhands coming in and out for a cigarette break, no one would find the closed gates an inconvenience. We convinced ourselves that commoners wouldn't be too interested in prying into the lives of masked men in the dark.

The clock struck the awaited time. I checked my bag for a knife and a robber mask among everything else. The pressure of it all got to my head so much that I forgot the reason why I ended up with a knife in my bag. One problem helped take the load off another. Whenever I considered turning the other way, I remembered to remember my net worth. To remember how many years of saving would get me a thousand dollars. To remember the promise made and to remember how it feels to break promises. To remember that we chose violence because we had to.

I fought a spiritual war when there was a valid reason the whole time. To help me out is one. But to actually suggest a stupid idea and execute it for me because he was a little short of money, and because he was a little too tired of normal life, he was just unbelievable to me then. Certainly not in a good way.

Out of how many poor chaps in the country, how many slip through the cracks and go the other way?

• • •

"Let me live, I'll let you know." He responded a little too quickly like he knew this was where we'd get to. "Just let me live." In the heat of the moment, I'd bet a guy like him wouldn't be too sure if it was his wife's voice. Perhaps, a little more of my voice would only further put me in trouble. I had promised myself I was gonna go all the way in. Someday or the other, all these promises might just come back to bite me in the ass.

"Show me the money." I hid the knife out of sight, making sure to go through the rest of the night with as few words as I could. He loosened up a bit, noticing the gesture.

"Look into the glove compartment," he said quietly. "The glove compartment." He repeated himself, now, louder and bolder, very much like he always used to do in the office. Only reminded me more of how terrible of a boss he was to us. Devon opened the car just then. I let go of his shirt and himself, to lean in and get a better look at his personal life. Sometimes, curiosity wins over the amateur criminal's mind.

The inefficient street lamps did not make our vision any better. Following a moment of confusion, I hit the dome lights on to help us see better. The first thing on the driver's seat was a bottle of smooth whiskey and a corkscrew. We might have caught hold of a family man on his way to a household party. Without his money, there should be nothing worth celebrating about. Except for getting mugged, of course: a party to commemorate the single most interesting thing to ever happen to him.

I saw papers scattered around the dashboard in disarray, a classic ashtray mounted over the bottle holder that came with the vehicle, and all nonsense — from crushed plastic to food waste — strewn around the floorboard. Everything to my first sight was right out of a bachelor pad. Behind all the nauseating mess, however, his family's OCD might have got the better of him. The old guy's wild child lived only in the front seats.

The well-kept back seats, covered in and out of leather, had not a single noticeable spot as if Biscuit was exceedingly keen on making sure his wife sat only in places his rum bottle didn't sit in. For the downright difference between what he was and what he wanted to be, anyone could guess how sad his life at home would have been.

Did we really have to make a joke out of a half-assed husband pathetically cleaning after his habits of smoking and drinking every single night before he went to bed? Maybe, it is only the guys living a shitty life who tend to do the same to others. If they were sympathetic enough to at least let others have the life they couldn't get to live, their God would have been a tad bit kinder. Moral dilemmas helped me stop and question myself for jumping the gun. My conscience did its duty, effectively so, until the very last moment I opened the glove compartment, only to find money, more than what I'd looked for, stashed inside a brown envelope.

• • •

Two rules I laid around the night's incident helped me out of all grievances. For one, I was hurting no good person. For another, I was hurting, by myself. These two rules might have also helped me make reason out of my driving away with abandoned money I found inside eight red tubs.

Since quitting our jobs right away might arouse doubt, we had planned to leave the company, one after the other, sometime around the next two months. We had planned to maintain a low profile and not butt heads with Biscuit for whatever time we had left in there. We had planned to forget all that ever happened and to never take a look back at the night. However, as expected, all plans stayed on paper.

Nobody seemed to care about two people running through the gates with a mask and a knife. It could have been a murder if not two or more, and it is only thanks to such people, crimes continued to happen. Once a critic of the narrow-minded ones for not giving a fuck, I was now put in a position to feel grateful they never change.

The Kindling

CHAPTER V

Undue Diligence

October 17, 2007

"Guys, when do you plan on getting out?" The driver asked, after having stayed quiet for half a minute. The sun beat down the main road at 80 degrees. Between a week of chilly temperatures and sudden downpours, it was the hottest day in a while. Sweat: dried and undried, had settled under the shirt. The day's climate meant no place for rainfall.

"So, you work here, J.J...." he read the name board with doubt to make it clear he hadn't heard the name before. "... Designers, yeah?" I nodded. "Are there any jobs to fill? Anything you think I could be useful for?"

Without notice, Devon got defensive. "No, not really. We're thinkin' of quitting ourselves." He responded crossly, getting out of his seat. "We are?" I asked in his ear.

Quitting only after the night we found the big bucks wouldn't look too good. Before boarding the taxi, we had only planned to spend the workday's time like we would have had nothing happened the previous night. To think about how different everything would have been — had nothing, in fact, happened — was already a feeling so ridiculous. No one can help me imagine how ridiculous it feels now that I can see everything I couldn't see at the time.

"We should have quit a lot earlier, why not now?" he replied, before finding his way in. We had an unplanned meeting every evening at the cafeteria. It went without saying it was gonna be no different this time since nothing apparently happened last night.

Now that I'm talking about the money anyway... when you own what I own, you can't really do anything to forget about it all.

Whatever is happening to you, it stays on your mind. You can try and think about other things, but it still lingers in some corner of your mind for as long as you keep the money. Fortunately, my day ahead threw in my way enough things to worry about. Thanks to the maniac of a boss I'd got, the money lived in the corner for longer than it did not.

One meeting after another kept me busy and away from my phone. For as long as I was away from the phone, I couldn't have called Devon nor could I have answered his calls. For as long as I didn't receive his calls, I couldn't have received anyone else's calls. And that ended up a problem I didn't see coming.

I saw myself pacing towards the cafeteria, without it looking like I was rushing. I figured running would make everyone suspicious, inviting unwelcome attention. In hindsight, running should have looked a lot less weird.

"Woah, woah, what's the matter?" Devon asked, as soon as he found me on my feet. I caught my breath, also secretively. I turned to the other side, my palms to my mouth. "Don't give me bad news, Cody." He spiraled. For a few seconds seemed too long for him to keep calm.

"Not sure if it's bad news." I passed my phone to him. He had, surprisingly, held his fort quite well since there weren't any missed calls on his front. There was, though, one guy who tried calling me an hour before. And since J.J.Designers took pride in not letting their employees use phones in meetings, it was only at the cafeteria everyone caught up on missed calls and text messages.

"Jonathan? The security guy?" asked Devon, a little louder than usual. On getting the women on our side to turn their heads, he whispered the next second, like it would make any difference. "Does he call you ordinarily?"

"Yeah, he calls me every day... Why would I come to you if that's the case?"

"Then why did you come to me now? Go ahead and talk to him."

"I have no idea why he's calling me. He has never done that, ever! Devon, did we fuck up along the way? Did we leave any trace of the money?"

"Well, there's only one way to find out." He remarked. It sucked that he was right, but he was. After much hesitation, I dialed up Jonathan.

"Hello, is this Cody Mills I'm talking to?" He answered the phone in the first few rings only to begin the conversation before I did. It was always easy to talk to him since it was him talking most time.

"Yeah. What's up, Jon? You called me sometime before." Devon urged me to put the phone on speaker.

"I did, yeah. Listen, a guy came looking for you this morning."

"A guy? What guy?"

"A black guy. Tall and... half-bald... well-dressed, I guess. Had a suit on, looking like he was out for business. I told him you weren't here from the morning. He said he just had to see you. He didn't let me get to my business, man."

"Now, wait a minute, why is Jon still working the shift?" interrupted Devon, out loud, in an uncalled moment of self-realization. Jon could hear. I put the phone down impulsively. Just as it looked like we were getting somewhere, I hung up on the source, hoping he didn't hear as much as I did. Not clever enough to read the room for a second, Devon went on with his speech anyway. "He was there when we took the truck in, he was there when we came out. He shouldn't still be working, how did we miss that?"

"How is this really crazy enough to cut him off like that? Can't you wait until he stops talking?" He shook his head innocently. "Thanks, man. Now, thanks a lot." Jonathan did not hold the most important of jobs and not everyone was as regular as he was. When the others were late, he worked longer shifts. He took home extra money. It was how things worked back home. But I wasn't gonna sit him down and explain things. "And now I have to do it all over again."

The phone rang on its own and it was Jonathan again with zero self-respect. We looked at each other in disbelief. I couldn't feel too bad though, for all he did was make it easier for us. "I'm sorry, please go on." I said, before which he had already begun.

"He said you have something he wants. Can you hear me? He wanted to see you so bad I called you up to let the two of you decide things for yourself. But you didn't pick up, did you?"

"Oh, crap. What'd he do then?" Ledger looked toward me with interest so I would put the phone on speaker again. I turned my back to him, which should have only been done already.

"Nothing, really. He waited around and left the place saying he'll take care of it. Gotta let you know, Cody, he looked a little pent up."

"He didn't give you his name?"

"Well, I asked him. Twice. I mean, you know me. You know I would. He just wasn't too interested in telling me his name." The security guard began working his way to the truth. "Now, is there a problem, Cody?"

"Alright, thank you, Jon." I hung up, choosing to go deaf.

• • •

For the taxi ride back, it didn't matter who could hear us speak. No time was good enough to plan ahead. Listing down every guy who fit the description didn't do us enough favors. From the day we ripped off Jerome, Devon and I worked hard and late most nights for make-believe reasons to keep us off the suspect list. We were also the only two working late the night before. No one was ever allowed to enter the locked garages. No one ever had its key. I had to capitalize on how empty the building was, coincidentally or not.

It was nobody's guess we'd find the forever-locked garages open. It was nobody's guess we'd find eight red tubs full of one-dollar bills in a truck. At least with the key already latched on to the half-opened door, it was pretty clear the truck didn't fall off the sky. Yet, it was all set up so naturally for us to be convinced it did.

We reached Devon's place in time. With no tall, suited black man in the vicinity, we rushed inside, shutting the door behind us. "Basement's locked. The door, still locked. We must be in the clear." He ranted, as he toyed with the lock and key, thanks to his sweaty hands.

"I have to see things for myself. Unlock the door!"

Every second between the door opening and the lights flickering, I could only imagine the money going missing every which way. The lights flickered for one last time before hitting the center of the room. I raised the carpet folded around the money containers for extra protection. Déjà vu hit me hard: The cash — all of it — out in the open again, under Ledger's roof. His basement proved more safe than my entire house did.

"Gosh, I need a cigarette," were the first words out of my mouth after seeing the boxes, safe and sound. I popped up a gum immediately to keep my mind off smoking. Not a day after I smoked a cigarette for the first time in a while, I was already on addiction killers.

Devon turned down my offer of one. "You'll want it. I'm allowed to smoke." He paused, already getting back to positivity. "Hmm. Cody. What would you've thought if someone told you a few days ago we'll find a goddamn treasure? A goddamn treasure stashed inside the parking lot of a company going bankrupt: how crazy is that?"

With the security cameras going kaput, and having the whole building to myself, I couldn't resist but do things I could never do otherwise. One day, I had my dirty shoes on Daniel Jenson's favorite seat in the conference room. On the other, I worked from Jerome's chair. I wouldn't have thought twice to maybe try and take his things home. People were at least clever enough to lock all drawers and storage units.

The day I had nothing on my calendar except a stroll through the restricted areas, I saw the truck and I saw the money. We couldn't know how many days the money had been sitting there, waiting to be found. "No. Of course, I would have laughed." I replied hesitantly, in two minds. I turned to my inner voice. You know what'd have been even better: Had I been all alone the previous night.

Lightning and thunder blasted the midday sky already turning dark. We heard raindrops from ten feet under the ground level. Time spent underground didn't make things any better. Devon began running up the ill-lit stairway, passing orders that failed to reach me over all the wet winds gusting through the open windows. I presumed it was about time to bid goodbye to my wealth. I rewrapped the useless carpet, still preferring to spend the day watching the money up close.

Devon scurried right and left, closing one window after another. "Can you come and help me?" It was him frustrated with me, now that raindrops wetted his wooden flooring. I made my way up, padlocking the stockroom door for good. I looked at him up and down as he marched in a hurry. Where to? Clueless as I was.

"Man, stop running and tell me: what really is the agenda? Where do we go from here?" I asked. Since it wasn't right to sit around, watching the money, doing nothing, I wondered what the right thing was. We did nothing with our lives but put off one fire after another. Ledger stopped to think, letting raindrops dot the windowpane for a few seconds.

We sat down to plan for the first time. Since it wasn't for us to figure out who we were running away from, it was important we at least figured out where we were running to. "I mean, you can't move cities with a buttload of cash. Can we somehow find a way to bring it down to one tub?" I asked.

"How do you do that?"

"Well, you know, obviously not by ourselves. Man, it's all full of one-dollar notes. All of it. Is there no one who could give us hundreds and thousands? Not a bank, that, I know."

"Are you ballsy enough to meet with a criminal, Mr.Mills?"

"Well, I don't know what we are now."

A sit-down conversation without one pushing down the other was what we needed to feel better about ourselves. I was afraid the money — with Jonathan to Jerome and everyone coming in between — was driving a wedge between the two of us. So much so that we could end up beating each other to death over who gets the bigger share.

In the middle of all the give-and-take happening as part of the moving-on process, *Tkk Tkk*: a knock on the door. The elaborate ruse Devon planned for us to go missing out of Cleveland's thin air hung halfway. *Tkk Tkk Tkk Tkk*! Harsher and quicker by the second. "Is this the guy your guy was talking about?" My partner asked, getting up and closer to the door.

With every further knock on the door, it was more and more clear we were not prepared for an attack. "Do you have something, a knife, a gun, anything?" I asked him in a hurry. He signaled me to wait and rushed inside. "Who are you?" I screamed to the other side to stall for time. The stranger banged the door even harder — not quite the expected reply.

Water seeped underway, reminding me of the rain outside. Nobody likes to get caught in the rain. Perhaps, that was it. That was why he wanted to break in so bad. Or she. I was finding reasons to not be afraid. With Devon shouting back about the knives he found in the kitchen, I should have probably waited for him to come and hand one to me. I was out of wits. Afraid the door would fall apart. With water flowing in, slowly but surely, there wasn't much left to do.

I opened the door.

• • •

More water rushed in. "Oh, sorry guys. I guess my boot's a bit damp from the rain." He took down his hat... and read the room with his squinting gray eyes. A tall black man with a costly suit: All of this wasn't enough for him to cross my mind. But how?

Devon walked into the living room with a kitchen knife in either of his hands. "Oh, fucking hell!" Devon gasped. I had already frozen in terror.

"I take it y'all know me. Partners in crime, is that right?" He laughed as if he didn't almost break into the house seconds ago.

"What-what are you doing here?" I asked, in a mechanically calmer voice.

"That is a good question to ask..." he said, turning to Ledger. "...without a knife in your hand."

"Jeff." He mumbled under his breath.

"Yes, I'm Jeff Walker. Pleased to meet you. He is Cody Mills, and you are... better speak up. You see, I'm weak at remembering names. However... they say I'm wonderful at remembering faces. You guys — for all the favors I've been getting from you... well, I'm not forgetting you any sooner."

"You have no business here. What are you doing? Why are you here?" I asked in a steadier mind, shutting the door behind him. "Why the fuck are you-" I couldn't go anymore.

"So, you wanna play it this way? What, you taping me or something? Okay, fine... First things first, you owe me an apology." I looked at him, confused. Was I only imagining things? Was he not here about the money? "You put me on the spot. You stabbed me from behind. You took with you the only copy of my speech and you flew away like a bird. What was I supposed to say to Jenson? How was I supposed to help your boss Biscuit see defeat? How?"

I shifted my eyes from one corner of the room to another, thankful for Devon being as confused as I was. The dramatic monologue he was just done with, was apparently his hit at sarcasm. Or that was what was implied from the way he grinned after a moment of silence exchanged. "Haha. Alright, jokes apart, where's my money?"

"What money?" I asked. Ledger closed in on Jeff, the knives still tightly held.

"Wait a second, I don't get it. What exactly is your plan? The felony for what you've already managed to do itself is sizable, now you're planning a murder." He replied strangely calmly.

"I don't know what you're talking about. Can you please get out?" I asked. He continued to stand there, pat drying himself on one hand. Checking his bag for something on the other. He didn't stop until I continued. "How is it your money? I wouldn't keep money in a locked-up garage. God knows what you did to get it there."

"How did you know about the money if the garage was locked? Or, do you just pry open locks when you get bored?"

"Well if you..."

"None of your damn business." I interrupted Devon. He looked at me, feeling humiliated. He had to know I wasn't gonna let him spill the beans to a new company.

Jeff noticed the tension brewing between the two of us. He made sure we noticed that he noticed with that annoying smirk of his. He moved around the room, taking off his coat, and his shoes, his bag on the table, raindrops drooping everywhere inside. The bossiness didn't lose him in the new avatar either. But the Jeff everybody knew of, was reserved but sophisticated. Not a creep-inducing grinner. From shuffling through his backpack to his coat pocket, he kept himself occupied until one of us had to fill the room with words.

Of course, it had to be the betrayed Devon Ledger breaking the silence. "Mr.Jeff, I'm Devon." He dropped the knives on the couch. "I don't think I have anything to do with whatever you're talking about. We have an office meeting going on. Important one. Do you think you can do this some other time?"

"Wow, Devon. I'm honestly blown away by how you're talkin' all cute and ignorant — like you just didn't rip me off my fucking money." I contained a laugh, struggling to believe if he'd actually thought that would work. We exchanged a silly look, which he noticed. Again.

Devon couldn't stand but crap his pants on the very first level of repercussions. He's as tough as they come. I was tough, though. Rid of courage, he wouldn't last a day in the crime world. He tried though. He tried again, tried his best to show me he was good. "Jeff, we're nobodies. You're wasting your time here."

"What the fuck-who are you man? Don't make this about the two of you. I'm right here asking for my money, and you're all about winning him over. You idiot!" He sifted through the third zip in his bag and pulled out a goddamn revolver.

"Devon, you shut your mouth. Speak no more." I said, throwing my hands in the air. Ledger dropped to the couch — whimpering — as we went about the conversation. "Listen, I'll take you to the money, don't do anything crazy."

"You don't take me to the money. You show me the money. I know it's in there somewhere. I saw the truck outside."

I had to be quick. I had to think on my feet. I had to make up bullshit and sell it so well he buys it. "Look, the money is in my house. You..." He shouldn't know I got tipped by Jonathan. He would only believe me less. "I live in the east. It's an apartment. I'll take you there, you can see for yourself." Some truth only helped the lie. He knew I wasn't lying. I knew I shouldn't be, for my plan to work. He paused to think. Actually.

"We unloaded the tubs at my place — all eight of them — and parked the truck here so no one could find out. That is the full truth. Please, drop the gun. I don't wanna die over some stupid money."

Jeff Walker lowered the gun and looked at Devon to see if he agreed. He was mindfucked. He couldn't believe I could come up with so much so quickly. Whatever be what he actually thought, Jeff bought it. He assumed Devon was angry because I gave the truth away. For once, his irrelevant reactions paid off. Jeff smirked again, so proud of himself.

"Devon didn't lie. We do have an important meeting. It's with Daniel Jenson. It's on the office calendar, you should know. We don't wanna make anyone else suspicious, do we? You can stay here if you want to. We'll come back in no time."

Asking him to stay only further cemented the idea that the money was elsewhere. Thank goodness, Devon didn't speak a word. Whatever kept him quiet, we were winning. In hindsight, his stupid antics did come in handy. If not for his half-assed attempts at fooling Jeff, things wouldn't have come together all that beautifully.

"No, I don't trust you," said Jeff, "I'm coming with you. No, you're coming with me. To the office, and then, to your home. Hand me the money, you'll walk alive. You pull off something shady, you're not gonna wake up tomorrow... Now, walk out of here like there's a gun up your butt."

CHAPTER VI

Man Escaped

[CENTRAL NARRATION PLAYS]

It is unusual per se for this to happen with no knowledge of any other inmates. Perhaps, a purposeful unfriendliness. Perhaps, an unbelievably close-knit pack of gangbangers operating inside the four walls. If it's the latter, then who's going next? Two officials suffered a blow to the skull. The rest were unharmed in every way. A not-so-typical prison break. Zero leads.

Detective Thomas Lee leads the investigation. The escapee sneaked to a blindspot seconds after breaking out, after which he allegedly fit himself through a tiny gap that could have launched him into the woods. The hand-made dagger with which he took down two guards had his thumbprints embossed all over it. But a voyage into the jungle at two in the night could never promise us if he did make it out alive.

Lee's instinct tells him the bandit is still at large. He feels the pressure to rustle up a significant lead. If not, the Feds take the case home. A first-degree misdemeanor for which he could have gotten out anytime in the year. Why botch an easy take? Unless it was a must to get out early for something so urgent. What could be so pressing as to make him break out of a prison full of petty offenders despite knowing he'd leave trails all the way out? Detective Lee knew something was off-putting. What was that *something*?

"Pick up the search warrant from the court, it's getting ready." Thomas schooled his four-member squad on his way to the prison in question. "Susanne: the runner's place in Sixth Avenue, Justin: the outhouse in Slavic village, after which... I need both of you to go to his parents' place. Two better than one in that case."

He caught sight of his uninvolved crew agreeing with him glibly. He raised his voice. "These jailbirds would probably shit the beds after a crime of this degree. So it's very possible he's all over his momma's lap right as we speak. If there's no questions — we're going all out." He turned his back and started walking before any questions were raised.

• • •

An unaccompanied Thomas ingressed into the minimal security jail, while the rest disintegrated on the spot.

It was an elliptical waiting area explicitly deficient of a rectangular door to be mounted on the barren hinges. A putrid stench of urine surpassed the unopened passage to the lavatory. It wouldn't pose a complete shocker if the lean middle-aged man lying on the wooden slab had already been suffocated to death.

"Excuse me, mate..." said Lee, hesitantly poking the man in a trance. "I'm looking for a *Henry Dickinson*, the jailer..."

The man bounced upwards at the intervention of a tall threatening man with a gun strapped to his pants. "...Henry? He's gone outside for a puff. Can I take your message?" His instantaneous shift in energy earned a smile from the policeman.

"Nah, that's cool... And, you are?"

"Luca. Nice to meet you."

"Same here, Luca. You work here?"

"One could say that." The cop nodded to him haughtily, examining the room. Luca dug his own grave, attempting to fill in the silence. "... I mean I'm a convict... From one-not-six."

Thomas pulled out a 9mm from his holster and pulled back immediately. "Get up. Hands in the air... How did you break out?"

"Whoa, whoa! Chill out, man!" he exclaimed instantly, holding his hands in the air anyway. "That fat bag Henry's behind this. I do this job for a month now. He goes out to smoke, he lets me come out. That's everything to it."

Fat bag Henry rushed into the arena instigating cigarette odor to an already pungent atmosphere. "Why would you let a prisoner do your door duty? Are you nuts? He's ten feet away from outside — if it's up to him, he'd escape in a heartbeat." Lee didn't make the effort to put down the revolver. He was now holding it against an experienced jail guard.

"Take out the gun, detective." He said boldly, warding off the revolver. "Get inside, Hacker. I'll take care of it." His eyes had in them a complacency.

"Hacker?" questioned Thomas.

"Luca. 'Hacker'. Johnson. His street name. What's the matter with you?"

"And you don't think it is... unprofessional to call an inmate by his street name?" asked Thomas with a critical eye.

"Watch your words, mister. I'm fifteen, if not twenty years senior to you. We're not dreamy like cops. We live with murderers and chain-snatchers. After a point, you couldn't help but float in realism." Henry Dickinson's words were diplomatic but his voice was stern. "What world are you on, pulling out guns at midday?"

Luca left the scene. And along with him, left one of the few foul smells. Thomas wasn't prepared to debate any longer. He was not ever a spontaneous speaker. It was something about the way Dickinson made his points making it difficult for Thomas to argue against. He strapped the gun back to his waist, behaviourally conveying a withdrawal... His *conscience* didn't give in though.

"... Just 12 hours ago, mind you, a prisoner broke out of here. I don't need to come out to these slums if you do your job right... What kind of jail do you run with the inmates wandering around like it's their dad's house? With this level of freedom, they are *definitely* breaking out the first chance they get. If criminals keep absconding, then, really, what good are you so-called *veterans*?"

Henry blew out a full ring of smoke. "Ah!" A satisfaction: it gave him. "First of all, Keith escaped at midnight. I don't do night shifts... Secondly, Hacker's not the kind who'd long to be outdoors. He's been inside ever since he remembers..." said the veteran. "Look here, buddy, let me make something clear. This is *my* prison. I'm in charge of it. And I know full well how to run the place. So... let's start over with 'What can I do for you?' or fuggedaboutit and leave me alone."

Following an exchange of loud silence, "To what pleasure do I owe this meeting?" asked Dickinson, choosing to wipe the slate clean.

"Keith Warner: I want the runner's profile and everything you have on him. The detective, who worked this case earlier, quit the force. I'm in charge now."

"I don't mind. It's on the computer. The window should be open. Take a good look at it yourself." responded Henry relievingly.

"I asked for a hands-on record. Not some computer. Don't trust machines. Never did."

"Man, what difference does it make? Are you from the past or something? Make do with what you have... By the way, if I remember it right, he is Keith Warren. Not Warner."

"Hey, you're apparently the go-to for these criminals. Excuse me for working on the good side of the law. I'm going after a man who's caught dead to rights for stabbing police officers. Worst case scenario: the victims he stabbed slip into a coma, says the medical report." Thomas Lee sat down at the computer.

• • •

"So, Henry, which cell was he in again?" After five minutes of unproductive scrolling, the policeman rose sharply. "It's better if I personally take a look at it."

The jailer, blatantly mad at the incessant interruptions, cast down the daily newspaper. "... In a minimum security prison, we don't have cells. We have rooms. *Dormitories*." He was visibly sick of answering to a cop familiar with not a thing about prison operations, yet, what troubled him more was the latter's disinterest in learning about things at least then.

"I see... Room number, it is."

"His number's on his file... Clear as day. Didn't you look at it all this time?"

"Well, of course. Of course, I noticed. I-I forgot. Just tell me."

"Y'know you're an awful liar, Cop." He commented, vaguely showing off how his name was as irrelevant as Keith's — to remember by. “One-o-seven.”

“One-o-seven... Why does that strike a chord... Oh, now, wait a second. 106 and 107. He’s a neighbor to this guy Hacker?”

“Great catch, Sherlock,” remarked Henry sarcastically.

“Well, okay then. Sounds interesting. Let’s pay a visit to both the *rooms*, shall we?”

“In fact, he might have been pals with Keith, from what I know.”

“Is that right?” asked Thomas. The duo advanced together to the inmates’ block. Two hundred cubic lock-ups aligned on either side of the corridor from start to end. The patrolmen — settled at the midsection of the two-fifty-meter hallway — were playing blackjack for chicken feed. The building was not a stranger to disturbing verbal abuses. They shared subtle eye signs at the entry of a well-built plainclothesman. But no one paused their play. “That’s yet another reason for you to not assign him door duty. We could have lost an important suspect for the case,” said he, after some thought.

“If it ain’t for me, you wouldn’t call him a suspect in the first place. Let alone talk sense into me.” Almost all the convicts leaned against the barred blue doors spectating the game. And almost half of their palms had gotten a hold of a cigarette of some sort. Marlboros, Newports, Camels, and rarely, handmade Cuban ones. The rest of them were either tired from smoking all day long or were not heavy on the cash front.

A hairless head shoved into invisibility, a few steps away. “One Hundred and Six. I can see you. Get out, Hacker,” the cop called loudly.

“I didn’t do anything,” he called back. The uniformed officers paused the game to get a look at the scene unfolding. Dickinson took a seat at the center table pouring himself his evening drink way earlier than usual. “Gentlemen. All eyes here. Your job right now is only to gamble. Alright? Now, cut me in.”

Thomas unlatched the door. The guards glanced out of the corner of their eyes. Hacker had fit his anemic body in the corner of the narrow dormitory. The floor was strewn with cigarette butts. A blackish powder had deposited between the bumpy gaps in the flooring. The detective clipped his nose on seeing a ramshackle of a toilet commode reposed very next to the sleeping area. This was the youngster's first tour of a jail cell, and he didn't pick the best of the lot to barge into.

"Dear Lord! Get out, for chrissakes!" he screamed, kicking the air. Hacker egressed his dormitory inching along the dirt-clad tiles. "I won't step out anytime after this. Leave me alone, sir." Poor Luca, dearth of any societal understanding, thought he'd lose his life over a silly interaction back at the entry point.

Thomas Lee followed him out of the nasty cell. He re-latched it for good. "Ah! Uhf-- Uhh!" he caught his breath, fighting off an incessant cough. "... Good God! You think I was gonna kill you? What, are you crazy?"

The prisoners killed for such drama. The inmates from the other side were already sincere audiences. The ones from Hacker's row tilted their necks against the rim in every direction, yearning to catch some of the action. Luca stood motionless. He felt so stupid. None of his excuses could make it up. "What business do y'all have with me? Get back to whatever you were doing." Thomas's words did no damage to the compelling audience.

The jailer jumped in, suspending the card game. "Mr.Lee, that's enough. Does it ever occur to you to take him back to the visiting hall and have your little chit-chat?"

The copper, respecting the rhetorical sense, took his leave pulling away Luca by his hand. "Listen up, 'Hacker' or whatever. I don't have time for this. All I want is for you to talk to me privately. *Why* would you hide yourself?"

"My dear boys. Get your heads off the rails and into your lock-ups." A moment of no response followed. "... Alright, watch the game in silence," the jailer declared with resignation.

• • •

The visiting area was spread over a spacious zone, marked by tables and teal chairs. The cop and the crook slumped over two chairs in the corner of the empty room. The 18th of October was recorded as the coldest day of the month. Hacker shivered in his vest, gawking at the cigarette case across the glass table.

"Do you want it? It's yours..." Thomas pushed the cigarette case to the other side. "... on one condition." Now, the lighter. "Answer my questions. Cut the shit out and keep it short."

He grabbed at the cigarette case the first chance he got. Thomas Lee hesitated to react and rode the wave instead. Luca was afraid of him anyway. Backing off seemed to work best for him to open up without two minds. A disordered prisoner a little too much into his cigarette could go nowhere near breaking Thomas — a man used to uncomfortable silences. A smoke or two passed. Luca gave out eventually. "What do you wanna know?"

"Very well. What do you know about Keith Warren?"

"Keith." He looked down trying to remember what he knew about the name. Pretty realistic acting, to his standards. "He ditched the house last night. Killed two guards, I heard."

"Let me rephrase the question: How did you know Keith Warren?"

"Who says I did? I knew him as much as the other guy. Nothing special."

"Mm-mm. Fat bag Henry has something else to say..."

"No..." he cut the cop off. "Don't take him for his word. He overblows every little detail, that son of a bitch..."

"Okay, this you must know. What did he get picked up for?"

He looked down again, well establishing his nonexistent relationship with the runner. It wasn't easy to believe he kept everything to himself over the six whole weeks he was there. Thomas reckoned it was the right time to press harder. "Overspeeding, I heard." He chimed in at the right moment. "Few others tell me he did drugs. A lot of it. Nobody has a clear picture."

"You're partly right, I'll let this slide." Thomas said, before coming in with another question. "For the last twelve years, Rodgers Penitentiary has been a stranger to jailbreaks. Why do you think Keith broke that record?" Thomas Lee grabbed at the cigarette in Luca's hand, throwing it to the ground. "I won't take *I don't know* for an answer."

The criminal, so far so distracted in his approach, straightened his back, taking time to carefully think about the last question. Thomas continued. "Convince me no one's going next. Convince me this is a standalone incident, not a planned operation. But if I get to prove you're not cooperating and that you might have helped Keith Warren in escaping Rodgers, they're gonna make sure you get bumped up to a medium-security prison. Kiss goodbye to freedom."

"No... Please... No sir, I don't..." He broke his silence, choosing to never shut up again. "I don't want no problems with a copper." He was hunting for words that wouldn't throw him in a cell. "Keith was normal, he talked to everybody. From whatever I know, it didn't look like he was planning a job, really. But to be sure, you gotta talk to everyone he ever met in here. He didn't tell me anything along the lines of escaping. I promise."

• • •

Henry Dickinson showed the policeman out. Groaning in exhaustion, Lee made it clear his day was a waste of everyone's time. He had come with no partners thinking to himself his work would deserve all the credit when push did come to shove. A thorough search of the runner's cell only proved to accomplish naught. When six back-to-back meetings with the inmates didn't move any forward either, Lee couldn't walk out with a straight face. If only the lunch hadn't been so-so.

"Nothing worthwhile, I imagine?" the jailer asked.

Thomas curled his fists, seemingly his last attempt to hold it back. He looked around until he understood it was best that he unloaded everything off his chest before going back to work the case. "I only came here because I finally got a good case. I mean, enough with public urination I said, coming down here all alone wanting to solve the case single-handedly."

He looked back as they walked away from the building. Looked back at everything from pulling a gun out in the first minute to almost leaving it behind at the last. "No offense, this place is a boring dump. It's not even a prison. It's a safe house for clowns, not man enough to do a real crime." Henry looked at the raging young man all surprised. He didn't foresee Thomas throwing around words like he just did. "Sorry, man. I said no offense though."

"Hey, none taken." He said with apparently newfound respect creeping over his smug face. "So, what did you imagine would happen?"

"I don't know... I gave myself a warning and all, not to shoot anyone, say, they come at me in anger." The jailer snickered, possibly reminiscing how he'd dreamed his first day on the job to be. "They're all so boring. Nobody knows shit. Nobody has anything interesting going on. And they're afraid of me — a police detective who doesn't know what he's doing. Forget it, I never should have come here."

"Like I very clearly told you this morning, it is a minimum security prison. Full of non-violent criminals. The reason why security isn't as tight as you'd imagine. This guy — Keith Warren — attacked two armed guards so desperately, to escape. Something doesn't add up here. It's either he has a history of violence we don't know about, or something so bad happened in his life outside these four walls."

"Go on." Out of all people, it was the self-absorbed jailer making sense for Lee. Whatever said and done out of context could throw him off the track. Thomas knew that from experience. He made sure to stay put and hear him out entirely before interjecting his half-boiled opinions. For all he knew, Dickinson was his golden ticket all along. He nodded with interest.

"I asked around. The cuts he made on them guards — I might be way out on a limb here — were made with a steady state of mind so they don't die immediately. Maybe, I'm overblowing it here." The cop's expressions made him want to continue. "From experience, I've got a feeling he might not be new to violence. His work isn't as sloppy. I wouldn't call it neat, he could be in his offseason."

"I did think of all this." He interrupted, still with bad timing. Not as though his owning up to new theories like that had any right time to begin with. But this was Thomas Lee at his unapologetic best. “That’s exactly why I came down here. Thought I could rustle up some stories about his past.”

“No, hear me out. We’re surrounded by trees on all four sides. Apart from sweeping the area to see if he slipped up and killed himself on his way, there’s no good reason to waste your time here. Work the case from the outside. Work his personal life.”

“Alright, enough outta you.” He mumbled to himself. Thomas — on guard as always — caught Henry as he made his way to order around the policeman he had no business with. He tucked himself into his car, not kind enough to recognize the man’s effort. A clash between two egos never leads to an unwarlike ending. The engine revved, ready to take off. Although, there remained an unsaid set of words ready to sully the birth of a new friendship. “You don’t teach me how to do my job, Henry. No offense, again.”

“Y’know you can’t use that to escape every time you say something mean.” He shouted as Detective Thomas Lee stormed off to work on new findings, thanks to the good old jailer.

[CENTRAL NARRATION ENDS]

CHAPTER VII

Fourth Man

October 17, 2007

"Can you drive?" He asked me downstairs. I really had to master the art of lying my way out of things. I could only imagine how better the ride to the office could have turned out had Jeff ridden his vehicle himself instead of letting us take the front seats as he played peekaboo from the backseat — remembering to remind us now and again why he was a guy to fear.

From the time he learned to pick locks, he began his memoir — a rather interesting one. If we were to go to the police, he was handing us information on a silver platter... until he went on to talk about his days working for a road gang. We could say he was full of shit. I would go on to say he wanted us to — to understand no part of his story should be taken seriously. He was at least right in helping us feel worse than we did — about him — when we hadn't a clue about his origin story.

Devon was on the same page as me about words: speak none. We heard everything he had to say. We were scared when he wanted us to be scared and confused when he wanted us to be confused. Whatever part of him I heard amidst all the inner voices, I played along — in reactions and sounds. So long as he was convinced he had us where he wanted, I hoped he wouldn't be too keen to make us answer questions. Devon didn't break this time. Or, worse, he was in a separate world away from guns and cash.

At the speed of a minute for me and a second for my clock, we reached J.J.Designers. Jeff stopped the car five blocks away. "You came in a taxi. Not in my car. A taxi. Both of you walk away fast. I'll be there in just a matter of two minutes." Ledger rushed out of the car, leaving the door half-opened. "I advise you: don't make stupid moves. I'm always watching." He hurried away like he had been trying to hold himself from throwing up. But it was also possible all he wished he could do was throw up words.

"Devon!" I shouted. Jeff and I looked at each other right as I threw my hands in the air in confusion. I was easily a moment away from flipping off my accomplice. I straightened up from instinct. I had been so used to keeping a safe distance from bossmen. Life wasn't all that easy now that it was normal for people to suddenly become someone else. Not that a single night changed how I felt about him. I didn't particularly respect him beforehand either.

"I have a bad feeling your friend might do something stupid. Make sure he doesn't cost *you* anything, Cody." Jeff warned me. I ran behind Devon Ledger.

"Where the hell you think you're going?" The sound of fast-going four-wheelers interrupted my fit of rage. I tried every bit I could to scream at the top of my lungs before I punched him to death. "Devon, stop!" He didn't. Traffic lights turned green. Between busy drivers honking for their way and pedestrians ramming into each other, waiting for the lights to change again, I made it across the busiest road in the neighborhood.

I chased him down the lonely road to my right. The treed pathway — not large enough to let two SUVs pass by, one parallel to the other — ran until the office gates didn't mind. Closing in on him, I was more confident he'd hear me well this time. "Why did you run away like that?"

"You can't talk in front of him anyway." He mumbled, stopping to take a look for himself if I did really chase him all that way. "And... you already made a fool out of me. What do you want me to do? "

"What..." I leaned over to ease off, leaving my question incomplete. For all the air I pulled out and pushed in, Devon didn't break a sweat. He was as merry to go on as he seemed a thousand steps earlier. "What are you planning to do in the office, can I ask?"

"Nothing, what do you mean?"

"Since you're all walking and running with passion, I assumed you had something figured out for yourself." I said harshly. "Move it." I waved him along, breaking halt. We moved as one — I behind him — trying to, really, find out if living to see tomorrow was still on the table.

"I'm as clueless as you are. Maybe more. But talking strategy in the middle of the road isn't gonna help the cause." He said. "Where is Jeff, anyway?"

"Right. Jeff." Two possibilities struck me: He was either waiting for us to reach the office like he very clearly said or had already drifted off to my apartment hoping to run into a pile of money. I was prepared for his car to come through — beaming white neon lights — at any moment. "How sure are you that he's gonna stick to the plan?" I asked.

"I still don't get it. You say you wanna go to the office... And he doesn't object. I mean, if I were Jeff Walker, I would kill you unless you show me the money right then and there." I remained silent. This wasn't a time to fight for my cause. "And, I'm not just shitting on your plan, Cody."

"Sure, you are." I still continued, for a moral victory. "I only suggested going to the office because I wanted to get out of his hair. We're not doing telepathy here. Without a plan, we're weak. We're nothing. But I didn't think he'd join us."

"Oh, so that supposedly never occurred to your genius mind?" He commented hatefully. "Whatever be his master plan, we need to be in the office now. Supposing he finds out we're not in the office, he'd get his men to do us dirty." He made sense. He could always make sense. If not for him losing control in moments we needed control, I never, for once, eyed the chance to become the brains. He's always been the clever one. It never bothered me until it did. Devon could have cost us everything if not for me. It's not very smart to act smart when your life's hanging by a thread. Anyone should know that.

Were we gonna call the police? Were we about to hire an assassin? Or were we gonna let in a third person on the shambles to further outnumber the villain? Then, what happens in case he gets to my family? "Yeah, you're right." I agreed with him.

• • •

We stepped into the bullpen on the third floor. Mild voices echoed in the corner room. Otherwise, there was no one to make any noise. Chairs were tucked into the tables. All lights but the corner ones, plugged out. Break room and waiting area, curtained up. Windows and back doors, bolted shut. A watery scent of floor-cleaning liquid filled the air. It was silly of us to have foreseen a crowd on a Wednesday evening after a thunderstorm. The light from the corner room shone brighter and brighter with time.

A fear engulfed me. We'd finally made it long after everyone left. But is fearing Jerome significant in the first place, when you've got a bigger fish to fry? I wiped away the fear in my face. When we were already busy preparing to face death, this was nothing in comparison. As we drew closer and closer, I began hearing two voices back and forth: It was a conversation. Not a self-absorbed monologue I assumed it would be. Did Jeff make it before us somehow?

We joined the two bosses having their evening drink. Daniel laid back in his movable chair with a leg on the table on which Jerome had his Cognac, sitting upright. But Daniel Jenson was always the first person to walk out of a meeting, always remembering to leave enough cushion time before and after meetings for Biscuit to kick us around. Jenson twisted around peculiarly, seeing two faces interrupt a private drink-off. He didn't seem very pleased.

"What are- what are you doing here?" Jenson asked defensively. Flushed and uncomfortable, he chugged down on the alcohol. Something seemed amiss.

"James?" Jerome tried.

"Cody."

"Ah. That's it! Cody. I didn't see you in the meeting." Jerome Biscuit claimed. "Where did you go? Your uncle's in the hospital again?" I had no answer that wouldn't get me killed. Jenson rose from the chair sharply. He grabbed his keys with his expensive-looking coat and waited for my boss to be done. He belonged to this or that side of the line, the *I'm Too Good* attitude flashing all over the room was something to comment on. He was intimidating enough for us to hold a respectful distance. A boss material indeed.

"Jerome, it's getting late for me." He interjected calmly.

"But you told me you'll stay back for another hour."

He sighed, very clearly directing it at the two newcomers that we happened to be. "No, I just remembered I have to go. Folks, punctuality is the best quality you can have. I'm disappointed in you." He told us.

"I'm gonna have to do something about these two, Daniel. This is not the first time. I'll take care of it, don't worry." Biscuit chimed in, fanning the flames. I was pretty confident he didn't know Devon's name. Yet he was as confident as I was in calling us out.

"Try and reform them, yes?" Jenson said before clearing the room.

As Jerome helped us with a show of hands, we sat down at the table against will. I preferred to think about the possible reactions Jeff could have when he found out I had fooled him. What was the worst thing that could happen, say we fled the city? Say we fled the state. Say we moved up to the upper-midwest to live out of tents. But I didn't want to die over money whose origin we were unaware of. It would be better to get caught, get slaught robbing the bank. But ain't it a disgrace to go without knowing what crazy crime we had committed?

"Why did you have to do that?" Biscuit snarled like a rabid dog. "Just as I am starting to gain his respect, bam, along you come! Should I fire you? What do you think, huh? Maybe I should. What do you say?" It was pretty easy to not give a fuck given that Biscuit and his company were the last thing on my mind. When having Jerome scream at my face did no good, it was clear there was no going back. We had to fight this battle until defeat.

I made up my mind to walk out on Biscuit with gusto. "Excuse me." A voice interrupted. It still wasn't Jeff Walker. "It's me again, sorry." Daniel said. "Jerome, kick back and relax. I need to talk with these two."

"Oh, no, no. Daniel, believe me. I'm dealing with the situation."

"And I don't doubt that. I know how commanding you can be. Some more authority on this matter will do only good, don't you agree?" Jenson waited there with a suitcase in one hand, his other hand on his hips. He looked at us with renewed interest. He who freaked out of the room on our arrival was now into *reforming* us, poor things. From his posture to his tone, he did a very good job of owning the room. Biscuit had to submit to him, of course.

"Come, take a walk with me, you two. Shake a leg, fellas."

• • •

For the better half of our walking spree, we didn't so much walk with the guy as much as we tailed him. That was the better way to put it. Jenson could have taken the stairs, taken the elevator. But he chose to go for the harder option: the longer way out. It seemed important for him to go all the way to the south wing and take the stairs at the back of the building. The musty corridors, the darkness, creaking crickets, and a sense of urgency: a tinge of familiarity teased me for a bit. Possibly longer-lasting than a mere déjà vu.

All the speed with which Jenson moved might have given Devon a taste of his own medicine. He looked back every five seconds making sure we didn't lose him along the way. The familiarity only powered itself until realization struck me. It was no déjà vu. Devon got it all figured out before I did. Strange though, for he only tagged along: an untimely associate I couldn't get rid of. I guess no one could really bring themselves to purge the mental picture of the haunting garage.

We were only a few steps away as Jenson made the final turn and looked back at us. What did it all mean? What does any of it have to do with Jenson? What happened to Jeff Walker? He questioned me before I could attend to questions of my own. "What do you think is on the other side of the door?" We kept our mouths shut for obvious reasons. It didn't seem like the best of ideas to own up to money potentially costlier than the company.

"The old garage. Hasn't it been closed down for quite some time?" Devon asked.

"Has it? Last I remembered, there was a huge lock on the door. Where has it gone, do you know?" He began showing signs of anger and impatience.

"No. I don't think I do. What about you, Cody?" My friend looked at me. I shook my head. It would have been easier to be mad at Devon for not shutting up. But I had to give it to him. He was quick and well-prepared — like usual.

The interaction with Jeff Walker: it was happening all over again. Only this time, with a guy of larger importance. With the money left loose in an unmanned corner of the office, I sensed it had to be tied to the office people in some way or the other. But having to deal with two of the biggest men in the office was something I did not see coming.

A gun cocked at my face. "Where is my money?" asked Daniel.

"*Whaat*-what money? Take the gun off my face!" Devon moved away, beginning to lose his shit. So was I.

"Cut the shit out." He yelled, pressing the gun down Devon's neck. "I'll ask you again and this time, give me the right answer. Where's my money? You know what I am asking you."

"Put the gun down." I cried. "Whatever it is, put the gun down. I'll talk. Put the gun down. Daniel!"

Holding Devon by his neck, he shoved him to the floor. Jenson pointed the revolver squarely at my face. "You make another sound, I swear to God I'll blow your heads out. You ripped me off over my entire wealth. You know what that's worth? For the last fucking time, where is my money?"

Spoilt Broth

CHAPTER VIII

Investigation

[CENTRAL NARRATION PLAYS]

Officer Thomas Lee pulled up at the spot in his refurbished van. Upon an hour-long drive through the deserted roads of the city, he could see things for what they were. What the jail guard had to say was valuable information. His words of wisdom came from experience and Thomas wasn't gonna let it go to waste. His associates greeted him perfunctorily for they had been waiting forever in the cold for him to turn up.

As most expected, neither did the runner's place nor did his outhouse prove to be of value. Carrying newly instilled inputs, Thomas was more confident than ever that he was gonna hit the jackpot with the last order of business: the parents'. He didn't bring himself to seek advice for nothing. At least for what he had gone through, it was absolutely important he be there for the interrogation. But was making four police officers wait by the corner of the road logistically wise?

"All this time, we could have been there putting the screws on his parents, you know? We've been right here for about two hours, what a waste of time?" Justin — one of the four angry coppers — indulged.

Lee got down from his car, pulling his collar up in reflex to the chilly weather. "Say what, let me hang around and have a beer or two. You guys can go ahead and see me through for a while." He commented, spitting his gum on the ground. They exchanged glances in response as Justin stared at Thomas Lee, this close to handing him a slap. Lee patted him nonchalantly with that annoying lopsided grin everyone despised. "It's a joke. Loosen up, everybody. I'm here now, ain't I? The more, the merrier. Come on, let's go." He declared.

A peachish hue tinted the surface of the buildings. The boundary surrounding the housing perimeter was fenced for an extra foot over the glass-peppered six feet compound wall rendering it impractical to trespass. For an ongoing police investigation, Thomas didn't have to trespass on any property. He still preferred to have all the cards. For what it was worth, he decided it was impossible for Keith Warren to jump over the compound wall. Had he taken the normal passage, there could always be eyewitnesses.

The squad passed through the gates, waving their badges to the vigilant security guard. The quarters housed six tall buildings in a cluster around the parking area. Every place in sight used to footfall was excessively roofed to the point the apartment buildings seemed dim in the daylight. Not a speck of trash marred whatever part of the manicured lawn looking directly under the sun. As though they had to work every day to maintain a sterile facade so something sinister could safely lurk behind. Possibly, it was only Thomas Lee desperately looking for ways to convince himself his hunch was on the money.

"Susanne, I need two of you to look through the place. We'll be up there going about our interrogation. Meanwhile, you'll be on the lookout for anything out of the ordinary." He declared to his partners.

"Tom, that sounds stupid. You're asking me to probe around a residential area because you have a feeling it might be a hideout. I'm not gonna do that."

"It's not just any feeling. It's a strong hunch. You gotta respect the gut when it talks to you." He gave up and looked around the three other options, finally totaling in on one of the two rookies available. "Fletcher, how about you take one other person with you and get this job done for me?" Fletcher nodded, looking at the angry Justin reluctantly.

"Alright, whatever. I'll be better off without you anyway," mumbled Justin on parting.

Thomas cast a shameless smile as Susanne turned her back on him. He stepped toward the rookie left behind and whispered,

"Hey, Theo. We could have scaled the place anytime. I only really sent them away so we'd have less crowd. Three is the right amount of people to intimidate old bags. Scary. But not too scary."

It had not been a minute since Thomas dropped the phrase *the more the merrier*, and he had already sent away two of the policemen. If three was the number all along, his partners could have put the last two hours to better use. But when it struck him that this could have been his golden ticket all along, Thomas Lee just had to be the man to get it done. Of course, if a new guy were to try and make such valid points, he would have been way over the line. After all, the perks of being under the line outweighed the consequences of any delay in time.

• • •

Since the old lady hesitated to let any of them inside without information up front, the cops had to invite themselves into the house. Thomas tried comforting the old woman as she seemed a minute away from making a commotion. His partners glanced at him in succession for his approval. He nodded his head as they closed the door behind them to eventually sit down without approval. "This is police brutality. I never told you to come in."

After allowing her to vent out the upset, Thomas interjected. "Ma'am, you're gonna have to calm down before anything. Surely, we weren't gonna talk in the hallway. This isn't what people call police brutality."

Tired of wailing constantly, the old woman sat on the hammock to catch her breath. The squadmates — generous enough to recognize the guy's manipulative propensity — played along. Thomas took a seat right by the hammock so he could bend over anytime to rub her shoulders. "Keith Warren is your son. Is that correct?" She stayed unresponsive. "Loosen up, Mrs.Claude. We're only having a normal conversation."

She bent down. "Correct." Stating an obvious fact to kick off a cross-examination was always the tradition.

"That's good. No pressure... Maybe, some pressure. So, when did you last see your son?"

The next reply came in sooner than he'd reckoned. "Two months back."

Thomas flipped his pocket note to go over the keynotes he had mapped out from his interrogation with Luca Johnson. "Did you or did you not visit him a month ago in prison?" The next reply did not come at all. "Did you or did you not-"

"Yes, I did. But he didn't want to meet me. So, you can't consider that one." She interrupted. "I'm not lying." Mrs.Claude added unnecessarily. The copper contemplated possibilities in his head, glancing over the two other visitors for a second. Theo, unable to keep it in, almost spoke a word before Susanne shushed him covertly. Love him or hate him, nobody could say Thomas was bad at his job.

"Where's your husband, Mrs.Claude?" He asked, rerouting the conversation.

"He's not in town." She responded quickly.

"Isn't he retired at this point? It's quite surprising he takes trips without you."

"It's personal business. You don't need to know." Lee nodded sarcastically. She chimed in again, answering questions that weren't asked. "Everything is good between us." She reassured him. "Just in case you wondered."

"Ma'am, you talk a lot about things I never asked you about, don't you?" He commented curiously. "Quite enthusiastic for having a son wanted all over the city."

"I'm sorry, what did you say?" She leaned forward, voice raising with every word. Susanne gasped visibly. It wasn't right for Thomas to let it slip so carelessly. Particularly since there was no ruling out that Mrs.Claude perhaps had no clue about how her son attacked two guards to escape jail. "What do you mean, wanted all over the city?" The woman asked carefully.

Susanne jumped up from her seat urgently. "Tom, can I talk to you outside for a minute?" She deemed it unethical, especially having put all faith and trust in him before the interrogation. As much as she wanted to bombard him with questions, she very clearly picked her actions so as to not set off an elderly woman. Because for one, she knew clear as day Thomas did no deed on accident. He wanted Mrs.Claude to hear it from him. He wanted her to put up a show so help him God see right through her.

"No, what-why did you say that? What happened to Keith?" She took turns looking at everyone from an uncomfortable Theo to a fuming Susanne. Her eyes bulged.

"What's happened has happened. What I wanna know is, why did it happen?"

"Thomas!" Susanne interfered, with Claude on the verge of a breakdown.

"Theodore! Will you walk this woman out of the room?" Detective Thomas Lee yelled out of nowhere. "I'm trying to have a conversation here." Theo watched the policewoman storm out in fury before catching the dead-eyed Thomas. The rookie fleeted to the door, joining his female counterpart for good.

"Your son has broken out of Rodgers Penitentiary and the Cleveland police are all about putting him back where he belongs." Thomas declared right after getting the privacy he wanted. Claude was ready any moment to let tears roll down her eyes. "Stop it, don't you put a fucking show. Maybe my friends are a bit too kind, but I've met enough people to know who's lying and who's not. You knew it already. I know you know."

"I don't-I didn't know anything." She said firmly. Only this time, there weren't any tears waiting for a cue. "Please, just talk to me. Why did Keith do that? I need details. You just dropped a bomb on me." She said impassively, trying her hand at changing the dynamics.

"Details can wait. Let me paint a picture for you." He said, refusing to take the bait she supposedly laid. "You're in your seventies. Your knees are weak. Your body's thinning. Not a soul gives a shit whether you live or die. Your son's rotting somewhere in maximum security. You — on the other hand — live between lowlives, chain snatchers, creeps and junkies. Every day, all day, you don't know what time it is, you don't know what to do to kill time. You're just counting the remaining days you have."

His squadmates took their ear off the door one after the other. To threaten an innocent (or perhaps not yet proven to be guilty) old woman for the sake of getting a confession was a bad omen. They couldn't know who was more dangerous between Keith Warren and Thomas Lee. Their friend helped the woman fulfill her words about police brutality. Or should it be said, *former friend*?

"I'm not gonna talk." She said, not with fear, but with disgust. She didn't like Thomas Lee. He seemed nicer in the beginning, but then his own teammates had to turn the other cheek on him. There wasn't anything she could do about it though.

"Okay." Thomas said, rising up sharply. His hands reached into his scruffy bag to pull out the first thing inside. He threw the paper folder on the center table for one last trick up his sleeve. One he wasn't hoping he'd need. "You know, I shouldn't have tried." The lad skipped his coppish attitude to sound defeated. Was Mrs.Claude sound enough to have read the laws about arresting civilians? Was she at least ignorant enough to not know that the police could and do lie in criminal proceedings? Whatever the case, it had to be tried.

"I'm not gonna talk." She repeated herself mildly.

"I know." He indulged. "I know that. But I wish you did. See, I was the only one trying to get you to talk. Not that I was the only one who cared. But..." He hesitated. Claude seemed like she could wait for another minute to hear the end of his story. She leaned a tad bit backward with Thomas Lee taking to humbleness. Things were starting to look up for the first time in a while.

"We came here to arrest you under reasonable doubt." His fingers ran past a few pages of his pocket notebook like he had something to show for his words. Where was he leading to? He had to figure that out along the way. All he could see was the name Luca Johnson flashing on every page. "Luca." He said.

"He was a friend of your son. Keith seemed to have trusted this guy a little more than he should have." He declared, folding back the notepad. “Rodgers is full of drug addicts, you know? Nasty people.” Claude paid more attention than she ever did the entire day. “Luca slipped up and gave us information. A little something brings you into the picture.” Lee put all his effort into making sure he didn’t come off as threatening. He was attempting to invoke sympathy from within. He smiled politely.

“No. That’s not possible. She looked up into the copper’s eyes. But this wasn’t a stare-off to achieve dominance. It was that of pity. “You’re-No, that can’t be. What are you talking about?”

“I wish I knew what to tell you, ma’am. I tried my everything to make you talk so I could at least convince my colleagues that you need not be put in a lock-up.”

“But, I didn’t do anything.”

“Doesn’t matter. All we need is reasonable doubt. We could put you in jail till we could say for sure you did nothing.” He leaned forward to hand over the document. “Once we take you in, the entire house is ours. Look at that, it’s a search warrant. We can do anything to get a shred of evidence that ties you to your son and his bag of cocaine.”

“No, Keith didn’t do cocaine. I promise you that. He was many things. But he wasn’t a burnout. He went nowhere near drugs. He was clean.”

Lee walked around the walls cracking his fingers, looking as nervous as the woman beside him. He had her. He knew it. All he wished was that no one barged into the house sullying the flow of everything he had going on. “Ma’am, with all due respect, I can’t take your word for it. He was arrested for possession of illegal drugs. We caught him in the act.”

“Bullshit.” She commented in the heat of the moment. “It was planted. So obvious. If you guys had looked a little deeper, you would have known. But no! You’re all about your arrest numbers.”

“How do you even say that it was planted?” She hesitated. With such a direct way of questioning, Thomas undeniably established that he was out for free intel. He had to come up with something and fill up the loud silence so as to throw her off the right track she managed to catch hold of. “I have notes from the prison conversations. Keith had been looking for someone to smuggle in contraband. It was many things from a cell phone to a hand-knife. Do you know what else it was? Cocaine. Don’t tell me they’re all liars.” It was the first time Thomas was flying off to somewhere so far from the truth. After a point, it wasn’t bluffing. It was straight-up fabrication.

“There was a growing rift between his gang. He didn’t feel respected. Someone must have plotted revenge against Keith. That’s the only way.” She’d finally blurted out information completely new to the police department.

“His gang, you say?” He paused. “Nobody told me anything about a gang. Maybe, you *are* leading me on to something valuable here, Mrs.Claude.” Thomas claimed supportively. Unfortunately, now it was way too improbable for Claude to not smell the policeman lurking out of the young man.

“There, now you have something to work on. Get the hell out of here.” She yelled restrictively. “You tricked me, didn’t you?” As much of a victory as it was for Thomas, it had happened at the cost of him losing all the respect of his coworkers. He was burning the candle at both ends but again, Thomas Lee wasn’t someone to get satisfied all that easily. He decided to push it beyond whatever seemed to be the reasonable limit, carrying nothing but blind hope.

“I didn’t trick you, ma’am. Believe it or not, I’m very much on your team. To be fair, two of my teammates were so done with my idea of making you talk they didn’t even make the effort to come up to your house. I don’t know what else would make you believe me, Mrs.Claude.” He said, before taking it further. “As good as what you say sounds, this isn’t gonna help you walk away. Luca Johnson — a reliable witness — gave me your name agreeing to come up to the stands to testify. What you’re doing is making claims in the air without any specifics. I’m sorry, that’s not gonna help any of us right now.”

“Keith...” She began, her hands in the air, her eyes closed. She was overcome with guilt. Possibly, guilt over giving up her son.

"Keith wanted to join hands with the Michigan bandits."

"Michigan Bandits?" A fluttered feeling shot up his egghead.

"They moved to Ohio a few months ago." She said. Thomas nodded to let her know she hadn't lost him yet. "Allegedly." She added.

"What about them?" He inquired. It didn't seem like the first time Thomas had heard about the Michigan Bandits. All the old woman did was probably give the lowlives a fancier nickname. "How's it that there's no record of his associations with them?" He asked in a firmer tone before realizing it himself.

She paused. With a second-long gaze into his eyes, she decided she'd shared enough. She turned away, walking towards the kitchen. "That's everything I know. Do you believe me now?" He heard her from the back. Something inside the policeman told him he might have stopped her from proceeding further. There wasn't any going back though. There was no point in sucking up to her any further. No place for talks about who's on whose team. "If you're still gonna take me in, I don't know what to say, young man." She returned to comment.

Thomas had already pushed the woman a mile farther past what looked to be the breaking point and still managed to strike gold. What more could a policeman yearn for? He should ideally walk away a happy man but, that, again, was the case a few minutes ago. There wasn't anybody to stop the man who could see no harm in asking questions.

It wasn't as though he could undo the shambles by walking away with what he'd got. Given that he was already neck-deep in shit to sink any further below, a little more shouldn't make things worse. Except, it was always possible for Claude to go bananas and pull out a handgun out of nowhere. It *was* Cleveland with no holds barred, he had to remember... But, did he?

"In my experience, ma'am..." Thomas indulged, with very fewer hours of experience than he made it to be. "It is when a witness says they've told you everything, they're withholding information. Leaning on all the information they've already given up, they hope to God they could get away with no one noticing the most important one they have in hiding... So, Mrs.Claude. Are you positive you're not holding on to anything possibly by accident?"

Before Claude could come up with an answer, and before Thomas could annoy her with a second question, his phone rang. It was Justin done with field duty. He swiftly picked up the phone to find out if it had been any worthwhile. He stopped. He reckoned he could make better use of the phone call. If he were to jump in with everything, why not all the way? "Hey, Justin!" He exclaimed loud enough for Claude to hear him.

"Yeah, man. I gotta give it to you..." He began.

"I won. She talked." Thomas said, cutting off his partner.

"Hey, that's good news." He said indifferently. "What exactly did you win?"

"You just can't admit it, can you?" He went about enthusiastically. And with that started round two of bluffing with Thomas Lee. Luckily, this time around, she couldn't half-guess he was making up everything on the spot. Not even Justin could. "Would you at least come up now? Yes, I'm not lying. We got information." Thomas continued with his half-baked idea mindlessly. The only possible conclusion the poor guy could reach was that Lee had probably lost it.

"Is everything alright with you? Do you want me to come up?"

"Of course, you're not gonna come up. You and your damn ego, it's winnin' over you, mate. You're not gonna believe what I found out." He winked at Claude so she could feel included. Thomas wasn't yet confident about his strategy. Most of all, he had to find out what he was trying to achieve with all this. Perhaps that Claude would eventually break — in the hope of getting the madman out of her house at the earliest?

"What the heck are you on about?" Justin asked as he should.

"You're right, it's not enough. Not enough information. But you know what? I'll talk to the captain. Who knows? He'll probably find it good enough after all." Justin hung up on Thomas, as most expected. Thomas had single-handedly rewrote the laws without being called out for it. It never should have worked. Nothing should have. He still couldn't get himself to believe old people were that stupid. If they really were, Thomas Lee had just the best day of his life.

"Mrs.Claude, how lucky are you? You might probably get out of going to prison." He said after putting the phone back in his pocket. "I mean, I sure hope you do." He declared, ready to leave the house. Thomas figured it'd be better for everyone if he wasn't the one scouring through the house in which he told the biggest of lies. A few other policemen were to be prepared to look after the search warrant waiting to be used.

If it was anyone in his place, claiming to have gotten the truth out of an old lady by treating her to an entirely cooked-up version of the lawbook, Thomas wouldn't have bought it in a million years. It was all very difficult to accept — as it was. Tempted as he was to turn around for a glass of water, he preferred not to jump over the likelihood of dying from poisoned water. The woman wouldn't have passed up an opportunity to slip him some rodenticide, he thought.

Thanks to his mind being consumed with ideas pertaining to all points in time but the present, it was usual for Thomas to leave behind belongings in the place of business. In the name of a customary tradition of self-inspection, he patted himself all over very subtly. The gun and the badge, check. The pack of cigarettes, check. The keys to his car, check. The search warrant, check. The tired lad yearning for a pat on the back for a job well done, check.

"If anything else comes to your mind, call me, alright?"

"The Michigan Bandits. Don't you forget about them, young man." She repeated herself like she always did. Even the hardhearted Thomas Lee couldn't help but feel bad about tricking someone too naive to fear getting locked up over nothing. All said and done, he still wanted to believe she knew nothing above and beyond the Michigan Bandits. On one hand, that would mean he did play games with an innocent woman. On the other hand, Thomas liked Mrs.Claude for some reason. As long as no bias obstructed him from doing the job he normally did, he was okay with liking a woman as old as his mother would have been.

He parted ways with Mrs.Claude en route to catch the elevator. He had to make sure nobody left home after the last phone conversation. Justin picked up, contrary to what was assumed. "Hey, Justin. It's Thomas."

"Are you sure?"

"More than ever. Sorry about that, I was trying to be clever. It didn't work out." He said, pissed with himself for trying to make a fool out of everybody to the extent that Claude could tell something wasn't right. "Did you wanna tell me something?"

"Aah... it's better you come take a look." He replied in the same tone he always used to. "The search around the buildings ended up to amount to something, after all." A better tone. Excited, one could only assume. Was it a matter to go nuts over, only everyone but Lee could say.

"What do you mean?" He asked, trying not to jump to over-optimistic conclusions.

"Come down and you'll find out." Justin laughed. Something he'd never do on normal occasions. Especially before Thomas Lee. Thomas abandoned the opening doors of the elevator for a much faster race to the ground along the balustrade. As was foreseeable, this was no normal occasion.

[CENTRAL NARRATION ENDS]

CHAPTER IX

Pandemonium

October 17, 2007

I was driving again. The roads were emptier than they ever were. I drove Daniel Jenson's Ford under his gun's mercy, tired of dodging his constant questioning. When it came to Devon, he hadn't uttered a complete sentence ever since Jenson knocked him to the ground. I couldn't know or ask what went on in his mind. I pressed down the accelerator.

"You better be sure the entire lot of money is intact. I don't want a single penny less. Do you get me?" asked Jenson. He, however, wouldn't find a single penny at my home, even if he tried. I obviously did not plan on taking him to Devon's place only to let him walk away with all his money and two dead bodies. But if Jeff, by some stroke of poor luck, was actually there in my house, all my master plan would do was aid Jeff and Daniel to discover each other. And it wouldn't take Jeff, if not Daniel, half a second to kill the two of us before he deals with the other guy. Somewhere, in the back of my mind, Devon, surprisingly, agreed to my words...

BONK! He struck the gun against my skull. "Do you get me?"

"Ah... Yeah. Yeah, of course, that-um... uh... Gotcha." It wasn't easy to look past the possibility of getting killed by my own boss. As much as I tried not to speculate on Jeff and Daniel, the more and more I ended up doing so.

Do they both even know they're after the same guys in search of the same thing?

What got me through it all — I hate to admit it — was what Devon would have preached had he not been a vegetable throughout: Dwell in the present, Cody. Dwell in the present. Dwell in the present.

From the way Daniel handled the weapon, it was very clear he hadn't yet gotten the chance to pull the trigger on anyone before. I was *not* up for being his first victim.

"Where exactly is your house, Cody?" His incessant attempts to break into genuine small talks further added to the unlikelihood of a criminal past. For the first time in two days, things started to piece together — I declared to myself: My boss could have been nothing but the owner of the money... which would make Jeff... Before I delved any deeper into my study, I reminded myself to answer Daniel before his gun made any contact with my head.

"Right outside the city limits. More or less, fifteen miles from here... We'll get there." I said, catching up to my train of thoughts before we grew apart. If it really was Daniel's money, why would Jeff come after me? Why would any sane person keep his money in a goddamn garage of an office where people come and go all the damn time?

Somehow, Daniel read the back of my head. "You say, you see money you've never seen in your life before, your first instinct is to steal the money, not making the basic effort to worry about crime, cops, or-or how it might affect the people around you." I further pressed down the accelerator. "No, it's almost as if my dad built this company for no reason..."

Devon turned away, looking through the window. And yet again, spread an air of silence.

• • •

It lasted less than a hundred seconds, though it felt awfully longer, for the gunman passed a command out of nowhere: "Park the car to your right." I seesawed my neck behind in confusion, continuing to move forward. He pressed the gun against my belly, tightening his grip. "Are you fucking deaf?"

I kicked in the brakes to save myself, causing everyone to ricoche off the seats. "Son of a...". Indifferent to all sorts of pandemonium, Devon made no fuss. As dazed as a level-headed accomplice is allowed to get, I frisked his thigh at least to ensure he didn't pass away.

My boss punched me ineffectively with his backhand. I curled and then uncurled my fists, reminding myself of the sight of a fat-looking gun sitting comfily in his arm. I guess I couldn't help but give away how badly I wanted to beat him until his pretty face disfigured. He slammed the barrel of his gun against my nostrils.

"You're too curious to know why we're parked on a land without a single soul at the very least a mile around us?" Blood. A drop of Cold Red Blood rolled down my right nostril. "Y'all see that well to your left? Well, one of you's gonna be pushed down that well before we move any further."

I pushed the blood up my nose. "Are you crazy or what?"

He hammered the weapon against my face multiple times, checking off everything I ever wanted to do to his nose. "I don't know, am I?" Amidst a mixed-up scene of violence and agony, I could still look past the clumsy bossman wreaking trauma on a man of flesh and blood reluctantly, only to come across an honestly harmless guy being pulled into a world he didn't want to be a part of.

I choked on blood bubbling from every hole over my face. "Hold up! Aah-you're leaving blood stains on my seat." He pulled open the door and pushed me out. My legs under the glove compartment, my head on the cold mud, my body caught in the air between. I saw Hell.

One of my many squeals crawled through, to catch Ledger's attention. He pulled himself inward dreading the possibility of a gun getting in his way. After a point, it's only the moving mental images sucking the life out of you. Neither blood nor twisted bones. I wouldn't go so far as to call it grief. But, it's this string of unanswerable questions and unquestionable answers. Including but not limited to: How the fuck did I end up here?

Right from when I seemingly stopped seeming as conscious to go through with yelling from pain anymore, Jenson turned to the second prey of his. "Let's let him be for a while. I wanna hear you talk." The barrel pointed to his ear. It could have ended there. A quick pull of the trigger could have stripped him of his life. But the coconut trees and the thorny bushes out the window, perhaps, meant more to him. His unresponsiveness bothered Jenson. Not even a good amount of blood could cloud my vision as I rooted for Devon to say something. Anything, so his head wouldn't blow up in pieces before me.

"Well, you're that brave?" questioned Daniel, pulling the slider back. "Everything but one! I believe everything from you *accidentally* stumbling upon my money to you *ignorantly* stashing it in your home, but one." The gun moved closer and closer to him. "I put the money in my vault."

Finally, it happened. After a thousand words were exchanged back and forth, one of those succeeded in making him look the other way. "Ah-hah!" shouted Jenson. "Busted! I put the money in my vault. Did it take a tour out to the garage on its own?"

I wheezed, getting the blood off my air passage. "Vault!" I howled as loud as I could, without bringing myself to choke on my own. No wonder they couldn't hear a damn thing. "What vault?" I howled again, spitting red saliva on the side.

"Well, still alive, aren't ya?" To Jenson's comment, I nodded, proud of myself for holding up. "Don't get too comfortable. I'll get back to you in a sec." Save now I had been put through far too much to fear his predictable punches. I managed to catch Devon's reaction as I snaked around in blood and sand. It, perhaps, reminded him of when our positions were swapped.

"If I don't hear a word out of you in the next 10 seconds, we'll never hear from you again," came the gunman's threat towards Ledger.

10... I was this close to giving away Jeff's name... 9... If Jenson had never imagined Jeff was on this money too... 8... it was not for us to decide Jenson wouldn't absolutely go mad and shoot everything in sight... 6... How would Daniel begin to listen to me if Devon would, forever, be a sitting duck... 3 seconds until Devon's brains were gonna be all over the dashboard... Ledger could say anything, for chrissakes.

A siren saved it all. A band of blue and red atop a speeding police van flashed from far behind. The sound grew louder and louder. The red and blue shone brighter and brighter. A hand pulled me up in the air. It was Daniel Jenson's. "... Drive along! It's the police..."

Cold Red Blood dripped all over his car yet he didn't seem to care too much. Me who needed another day of rest to break out of the comatose I'd been put in, couldn't press down the accelerator. Even if I were to, we'd only fall off a cliff somewhere to my hard left. It all happened so quickly. I could only process it all slowly. I couldn't fit in the chaos for I felt I was only a drunk observer. However, it all happened with me forming the centerpiece of the puzzle.

It wasn't surprising to see the bossman bend as low as the vehicle mats, assuming that the police cars couldn't see him if he hid well enough so he couldn't see them. But it certainly took me by surprise — though not momentarily — when Devon joined him in doing so. Despite knowing that that wouldn't do anything close to helping us evade a police van, I would have happily joined the party, had I been able to flap my hands and legs around without an ear-splitting cry for company.

Before Daniel could sneak a peek for the second time to make sure the four-wheelers were indeed driving toward our direction, the vans zipped through to some other place to take care of matters more urgent. All I could do was wonder if what happened was for better or worse. A vehicle with armed men would bring as much fortune as misfortune. To leave it at that was my easy way out. Once I begin to zero in on one of the two options I am provided with, is when I begin to make decisions that could potentially ruin my life. Or make it better. To leave it at that was, again, the easy way out.

Daniel raised his sunken head in disbelief. I'd go on to say he'd have cried at the sight of cops commandeering his sedan. He twisted his head to every side, his devilish grin growing wider with each twist. He pulled back and raised his hand, happy to know how he held on to his ownership of the weapon. Ledger slowly returned to his original position, as if we didn't just see him lose all cool and succumb to fate. I didn't move a hair until everyone and everything was restored to normalcy in a minute or two. Except for the guy in the driver's seat who didn't reek of a bloody face until ten minutes ago.

Though not with the same energy, Jenson tried his mighty best to start things over. "I've lost patience!" He added, as though he had any, to begin with. He leaned over to start the car and slapped my wobbly head like I was a bull ready to run off. I assumed he wanted me to drive again. So much more confident than I was that I'd not run us all into a lamppost, if not down the cliff. "I'm not gonna sit here and listen to the two of you telling me you didn't know how the money was teleported across two floors down south." He slowly tilted the gun to his left until I pressed down the accelerator again.

"Look, you gotta think! You're not holding a toy gun." Devon uttered a complete sentence with unbroken words after so long that it took Jenson a little while to believe it was only him.

"So, you *can* talk. Alrighty!" He commented in a frenzy.

"Maybe someone moved it to the warehouse. How would I know who?" He continued, in the very intensity with which we took off.

"I never asked you who it was... Now, I suspect you *do* know who it was," he asserted, visibly pressing down Devon's head further.

"Only you know who has access to your bloody vault!" He yelled back, still powering through with emotions, not half as concerned as I would be when a gun was *that* close to my brain. "I didn't even know you had a vault in the first place." Jenson paused for a while, unsure of how to proceed any further with the one-sided questioning going nowhere.

"You're talking to us like we're some seasoned robbers with an elaborate plan. We're rookies. We don't have a goddamn idea what we're doing next." I blabbered with great difficulty.

"I can't believe I was such a sitting duck ... not knowing a thing..." He groaned, slowly taking the gun off my friend's head. "... If only I hadn't gotten the *call...*" He mumbled again, in a voice almost indistinguishable from unintelligible gibberish. Thankfully, Ledger was at least conscious enough to make out the words.

He stared at me blankly. Almost as though it was something I had to know about. "What *call*?" Devon asked out loud.

"Huh?" The bossman went, beginning to realize he'd let words slip out, without control.

"You said you got a call. What call?"

"Hey, hey, back off!" He yelled, getting as edgy as a little kid. "I'm the one asking the questions around here!" My friend quickly turned around, to my surprise. Devon Ledger doesn't rest till he gets what he wants. If he wasn't afraid of a gun a minute ago, he didn't possibly learn to be afraid in the meantime. Jenson could have flipped his gun from one hand to another in relief. I could smell trouble coming from a mile away. If not this one, he's got another thing coming. But, what was it? I looked at the guy.

His eyes moved about sizing up every nook and cranny through the windshield in sight. Had he been looking for someone to spot the revolver between the two seats, he should have known that seemed a far cry at best. For the first time in a while, the bossman's words faded in the background. If at all telepathy wasn't made up, this was the time to know. I had to see exactly what Devon saw. I had to think exactly what he thought. I had to convince myself that he was looking for a way to communicate too.

Devon looked at me for barely half a second before turning back around. If that was all the signal he meant to exhibit, I had to think. I had to piece together why he needed a couple of seconds to inspect the road conditions before turning back to continue the argument he so casually broke off. A momentary glimpse at the steering wheel and its driver in between. No, he seriously wasn't gonna try what I feared he was.

"Cody, could you please help me find the truth here?" Devon asked, his eyes, still on the gunman behind. I could only assume it was go time. I looked around to make sure there wasn't any bystander about to plunge out of thin air. "Mr.Jenson, do you wanna know how the money was moved to the *garage* in question?" He asked animatedly, his hands out to air quote his words. Jenson, as expected, raised the gun, disturbed by the sudden difference in energy levels.

"Ten seconds." I said louder than I normally would. Because, from experience, more the pandemonium, the more chance we have to get away with it.

"Can you tell me who called you?" Ledger moved a bit closer to him, at odds with what anyone does under gunpoint. Daniel shuffled in his seat, charging the weapon but refusing to go further. A second of reluctance was all we needed to tip the scale.

With a twist of the wheel, I swerved the car towards the lamppost. Devon — without a second thought — dove back, throwing himself into Jenson. The violent collision of metal on metal sent shock waves echoing through the dark. Airbags blew up in the blink of an eye. Shards of glass had shattered everywhere around the battered four-wheeler. The two passengers laid heads over heels as their legs flailed about in every direction I chose to move. The revolver dropped to the ground.

Come to think of it, the airbags shooting out the gaps only made things all the more difficult. The inflatable balloons — as I remember them to be — did nothing but foil my face when I most needed to employ the sense of sight. With an obscured vision, I attempted to sense the door handle I knew was to my left. I gripped the window pane as sharp corners of glass pierced through my palms. I didn't have enough time to pause and feel the pain. After a great deal of cutting my own fingers, the door opened. I threw myself to the ground in relief.

Despite wanting to raise up and fight for Devon, the best I could do was remain under and mumble his name in oblivion. For all the blows I'd received, it was a wonder I could still see. But all wonders had to be overlooked when I knew I had to do anything but play dead. I couldn't bring myself to brush it aside, for it was the loudest sound I'd heard in a very long time. A gunshot.

CHAPTER X

New Findings

[CENTRAL NARRATION PLAYS]

Officer Thomas Lee stared at the parked car at the rear end of the lot with a furrowed brow. The vehicle seemed ordinary at first glance. Just another forgotten piece of urban landscape. Yet he was summoned to study the car in the middle of an ongoing interrogation. Wanting to have some fun of his own, Thomas toyed with all possibilities that could have aroused the hothead Justin to go so far as to make a call on his own.

At a distance, he noticed Justin breaking away from the group of four, finishing off a cigarette on his way. Susanne gawked at Lee from a distance, mouthing words only assumed to be curse words. He looked away, having had enough of her high-pitched squeaks all day. The thin layer of dust on the windows could only mean nobody used it for a solid day or two. However, in contrast to the other cars in the vicinity, he could make out the fact that it was either cleaned or driven in within the last seventy-two hours.

Despite wanting to go ahead and stick his face through the dusty windows of the vehicle, he'd imagined there was a reason nobody tried wiping off any smudges. Thomas held on to his horses, making all the speculations at a safe distance. "So? What do you think?" Justin interrupted the scene, asking exactly the question he was known to ask.

"I can only assume this car has something to do with Keith, though not directly related to him. It's better for both of us if you take it from here." He declared with a flashy smile.

"What makes you say that?"

"He's not crazy to not just stop at driving his own car, but also go on to swing by his mom's for lunch? Justin, the more I hear about the guy, the more I think he's not a rookie. Michigan Bandits and whatnot."

"What's the Michigan Bandit?"

"You don't know?" He asked, wearing a disdainful expression. To be entirely honest, neither was he all that aware of a gang going by that name. He might have come across the name somewhere. Couldn't exactly say. "They're pretty well-known around town." He added. Putting together dirt on this new gang was gonna be the first order of duties as soon as he made it home, he decided. "There's a chance he was friends with them."

"Keith?" Justin nodded with amusement. "Not bad for himself."

"So what do you have for me?" Thomas asked, cutting through all the small talk.

Justin circled around to the other side, inviting Thomas to follow. He wasn't used to giving direct answers, nor were people used to getting direct answers. He presented to Thomas, an unvarnished look at the windows under sunlight. The dust pattern on the adjacent vehicles — more often than not — seemed so much more complex and pronounced. One could only imagine it was the result of extended exposure. Justin picked up an ounce of dirt from either of the windows for further scrutiny. "Notice any difference?"

"What do you mean? No..." He responded without much thought.

"This is only mud. Sand in the air. The dust pattern in almost all of these cars parked here for more than a day is something like this. It's right about now when the sun settles in, we get a couple of dry gusts of wind. The wind brings in sand." Thomas nodded. It wasn't often he was really patient with what others had to say. "This car was only brought in this morning. At around seven thirty."

"There's no security cameras here."

"Correct. But there is a security guard. If it's not a regular visitor, the name and number are taken down. That's how I know."

Thomas ceased to continue with ease. He looked at Justin, holding his shoulders, wearing a face needlessly overdramatic. "What was the name?"

"Oh, grow up! It's obviously gonna be a made-up name." He remarked, warding off the cold hands clutching his shoulder bone.

"The number is fake too, probably. Don't think it's gonna be that easy, man."

"Alright, alright. About the dust pattern..."

"Right. Take a few steps back and look at this car. It's covered in mud from top to bottom. It's only possible it came in here looking like this."

"But the mud is thinner?"

"Drier. Smaller, too. It's from the desert. It's not local sand." Justin turned around, satisfied with himself. "Given that all the roads within a three-mile radius are good ones, the nearest wasteland is due west. Do you know what else is due west?" Thomas, having lost track of all the new information, whipped out his pocket note, like that was gonna help accomplish anything. He waited for words. "Rodgers Penitentiary." Justin declared.

"Rodgers!" He repeated, as soon as he heard half of it.

• • •

At around half-past five, the five police officers with fatigue etched on their faces, gathered around what looked to be a two-seater at the nearest restaurant. The day had been nothing short of a relentless pursuit, meeting too many strangers, and chasing leads, all in the hope of catching a darned jailbreaker. It was only fair to end it all with food and drinks, so they wouldn't think twice to do it all over again.

The clatter of dishes and subdued chatter permeated the hall hosting all sorts of people winding down after a long day. Six cups of coffee set in motion an ordering spree to appease the long-standing hunger. Of which, Thomas gulped up two. Holding the second cup for a last sip of the coffee, he casually insinuated his plan to review the day's events. "I wanna talk to you guys about what happened..."

"Whatever it is, it can wait." Susanne interrupted.

"Don't tell me you're still mad, this is important." He responded.

"Yes, I am still mad. Regardless, I'm not in the mood."

Thomas pulled out his pack of smokes, having moved on to a place only nicotine could come to. It was unfortunate for him, though. And needlessly embarrassing too, thanks to the police woman's scorn adding to the bitterness. For, the workers had to help him see the *no-smoking* board hanging out of focus from the ambient lighting. "Get a big frickin' signboard." He yelled, throwing the pack back where it came from. Only for the woman to smirk harder at the young man coming to notice a larger one on the opposite aisle. "For fuck's sake." He swore to himself.

Thomas preparing to get back one end, Susanne preparing to push him further down in the other, the waiters couldn't have found a better moment to barge into, had they tried. Justin used up the awkward moments of silence to their best, coming up with potential ideas that could divert the entire lot off-topic. Meanwhile, Theo and Fletcher, trying to fit in the circle on either end, had nothing to say, or do. To a point where they basically ended up ordering what everyone had ordered.

When no faces lit up even on seeing the hot food in hotter dishes, Justin had to interfere out of concern. "Guys, what do you think about my find?" He asked, glancing to his left and right, hoping one of the two rookies would take it from there. "We're gonna go back and crack open the boot like we talked about, what do you say?"

"To go from here all the way to Rodgers based off of mud prints in a windy neighborhood? I mean, wow. This guy must have rubbed off on you quite a bit." The mean-spirited lady commented, defeating the only guy playing for both sides.

"I'm out." He said with resignation and leaned away. "You guys are fucked up. Get your shit together."

It was Theo, choosing to go next. "I guess we could all just drink lots of beer and get going." Nobody agreed. Nor did anyone disagree. They all waited for lots of beer to make it to the table. It was the first time he wasn't condemned for speaking out loud. If anything did come out of the energizer session, it was Theodore out of his shell.

Once refueled, the officers resumed the chase, with a collective commitment to bring down Keith Warren and — at the very least — get a good night's sleep in the coming days.

• • •

It had to be the only time Thomas had ever used a crowbar for legal reasons. The security guard goggled at two coppers making it their life goal to pry open a car trunk. Just having heard back about the unsuccessful search at Claude's residence, other means were the only means. From whatever was already known to Thomas, and from whatever the red sedan gave away, they had to be creative. But again, it was all only based on the assumption that this car coming from Rodgers Penitentiary had something to do with the escapee.

The trunk creaked open. Disappointment awaited the crew as the spare wheel and the accessories that came with it occupied the majority of the space. All their attempts at bringing seemingly inconspicuous items to light ended with a reminder not to outsmart fate. The toolbox tucked away in the corner should have ideally hosted a set of lock-picking devices and a detailed floor plan of the prison he escaped from. Nobody yearned for it to be a regular toolbox. The same went with everything strewn about the compact trunk space.

Having picked up the sand specimen for Justin's sake, the crew began to examine the inside from the outside. Any empty, clean surface in the car was only seen fit as talking points for Thomas. To the policeman's eyes, it wasn't of use to clean the seats if not for blood stains and gunpowder. It wasn't of use to dust the mirror if not for all the sorry sights it had witnessed. It wasn't of use to discard the floor mats if not for getting busted. But, nobody really throws out the floor mats for no reason. With that, Lee might have been on to something.

"The floor mats! There are no floor mats in the front. You're telling me that's not good enough?" Thomas reasoned to his fellow officers.

"It could be nothing, though. Could be that someone threw up in the car. Could be that there *were* no mats to begin with." Justin declared in an exhausted voice.

"Yeah but if we're talking 'could be's, it could very well be that a shitstained Keith Warren got into the front seat, tired from all the running through the jungle." Susane indulged, in a weaker voice, if at all that was possible.

"Is that you on my team I see?" Thomas asked with a blunt smile.

"I figured we had a case on our back. My anger's not bigger than that." She gave him a reason to smile amidst the never-ending lethargy. He looked at everybody, hoping for approval, a nod or a blink was all he looked for. Justin had argued it wouldn't be clever to pry open the door like they did the trunk. With no knowledge of the owner, this distanced scoping was all the possible options within the window he'd allotted.

"You asked me for reasonable doubt. There's your reasonable doubt. I wouldn't rip out my floor mats to kill time."

"Yeah, but you don't have a Honda." Coming to acknowledge the silliness in his words, he looked away to see if there was anything that didn't involve breaking doors. "So, you're gonna use the crowbar again?" It was the closest he'd come to an approval.

Thomas gathered around the vehicle, the crowbar being the only weapon of choice. Everybody exchanged glances as the stout security guard stood by with a glass of water like he'd been watching a show. Now that they had come to realize he'd been hanging around ever since they came back, neither could they drive him away without reason, nor keep him close without concern. His eyes scanning the surroundings, the unbidden guard stood watch as Thomas inserted the crowbar into the seam of the driver's door.

It was the crowbar creaking in resistance, encumbered by the door holding steadfast against all intrusion. Though nobody offered to give a hand, he wasn't about to admit he needed help. He went in harder, exploiting the stubborn frame about which the weapon bobbed. A newly filled-up tummy was everything needed to bend the metal surface. Exactly what Justin feared shouldn't happen was permanent damage. On the bright side, the door swung open with ease.

Everyone crowded around the four-wheeler, each making up plans as they went about the operation. Thomas stepped back, watching the entire lot of cops go to work because he did it. He rubbed his pink hands triumphantly as he watched the security guard trying his best not to move a muscle. As regretful as the guard was for not taking up a closer position, he knew he couldn't try and sneak a curious look without risking the hotheaded narcs giving him a suspicious eye.

The car held nothing any normal car wouldn't have. It wasn't gonna stop them though, from overvaluing every article their eyes could see. Counting out the paper towels and sunglasses, loose papers used up the most space available. Gloved hands sifted through papers from the glove compartment, seat pockets, and even a few fallen under the seat. Counting out the vehicle documents, relevant physical evidence came down to nothing. Unless, of course, someone noticed the seemingly useless receipt Fletcher had kept aside.

"What is this?" Theodore raised a question, now that he could speak his mind, he decided. "Seems like a receipt."

"No, that's two months old, I checked. Just instant noodles from a convenience store." Fletcher replied, moving on to look for more papers.

"Give me that." Lee plucked it out of the rookie's hands. Upon a cursory glance, he could see that the grounds on which Fletcher pushed aside the square piece of paper didn't make so much sense. He looked at the rookie, deciding between taking time to yell at him and working the case. "It's two months old? A two-month-old receipt lying around in a car almost perfect in every other way, that tells you nothing? Sometimes, I don't get why there are so many cops." It was the least he could say. That he didn't get aggressive was good news for all. All but Fletcher.

"From back when Keith roamed around, a free man." He studied the contents, close to his eye. "Am I wrong or did he get picked up somewhere around here?" The bill included an array of details from the address down to the exact time. "If you're telling me the guy casually hung around there buying cup noodles at midnight, I don't buy it." He commented, staring at Fletcher with every word.

"Nobody told you that." Susanne countered.

"If he was there two weeks beforc the arrest, he might have been there every day. If he was there every day, we're looking at some kind of an operation, maybe?" His squadmates abandoned the futile search exercise to have a closer look at what was possibly the centerpiece of the puzzle. Had he been looking for a meal that late, he was perhaps busy all night doing work he couldn't get done in the daylight. More often than not, it's the covert operations that run in the night. If not anyone, Thomas Lee could see things take shape, having heard one part of the story no one else did.

"Fletcher." He singled him out. "I need you to find out the exact place and time Keith was picked up six weeks ago. Also, make a list of all the active underground mobs in and around the area. Preferably someone by the name of Michigan Bandits." Except for Justin, his partners blinked in ignorance. Justin blinked too, possibly to a lesser degree. For one, Thomas didn't take it upon himself to speak on the *conversation* that happened upstairs.

"Give it some time. You don't wanna know now." Because he didn't know shit himself. But of course, that shouldn't be the reason made public. "You've already got enough data up your head today." He said. "What I will tell you is that I got intel, he made some friends in the gang. It's possible they've moved to Cleveland only recently."

"From Michigan." Theo chimed in.

"From Michigan. Yes, thank you." The detective stared into nothingness as he attempted to map out the priorities in his head. "Security Cameras." He continued. "There's a chance there are security cameras in the convenience store. If anything, it's a green light we're going in the right direction. If we get lucky, we might even catch him with one of his accomplices." He cut his discourse short, before taking back the glimmer of hope he'd accidentally provided. "Although, I highly doubt he bought five-dollar cup noodles for more than one person." And that was every usable detail on the bill woven into their narrative.

• • •

It was high time the police officers focused on the discounted parts of the runner's life. If anything, they were only a quarter way in. Thomas was not up for taking the night to himself when he had an outlaw to go after. Regardless, his personal life wasn't as interesting as he wanted it to be. Sometimes, it was pretty much on the face he was striving to make his job his personal life.

"I'm taking the night." Susanne announced and walked off. She didn't seem ready for the partners to react off of one another. But she had to turn around and retrace her steps, for Fletcher gawked at her miserably. "I'm taking Fletcher with me." She put it out casually.

"Jesus, he's only twenty-two." Justin smiled.

"Oh, shut up man. I'm not in the mood."

"No, no." Fletcher interrupted politely, thinking up every word carefully. "I-I wanna take the night too." He said to everybody. "If that's okay."

"And, you can't speak for yourself." Theo commented snarkily. It was too soon. Thomas stared at him until his confidence crept back into his shell.

"Speak for yourself." He warned him. "Take the night. But I'll call you if something goes up." Thomas said to both of the leavers. "I'm afraid tonight's not a peaceful one." They had already come to a consensus without sitting together — Thomas was gonna talk probabilities all night long; and, it was some probability they chose to disbelieve until proven otherwise. More often than not, his forebodings remained on paper. But there were times when even the craziest of feelings had come alive. But there was no way to know. They were two heads less than ideal too.

Two of the cars began on their separate journeys: one with Thomas, Justin, and Theo; the other with Susanne and Fletcher. Susanne, with a minute-long headstart, revved up her engine and drifted into the horizon. With a smorgasbord of feelings and opinions — more good than bad ones — the crew took off to the next destination. The car was already halfway through the gate when Thomas decided to roll down the window and call the security guard.

The guard came running. "Yes, Mr.Lee. What can I do for you now?" He questioned. His exasperation was overt in the air.

"Sorry to bother you, mate. Can you tell me a little bit about the man who drove the red Honda?" He asked, pointing at the car they were just done ravaging.

"Oh." He exclaimed. "Sure... But I already told him everything I know." He declared, pointing at Justin in the backseat.

"Sure, yeah, yeah." Thomas agreed with him, only to get him to speak anyway. "I'd like to go over it again." It was a given Thomas wasn't gonna walk away unless and until he heard from the source man-to-man. He believed more the middlemen, the more the lost information. He wasn't wrong though.

"I mean, I gotta tell you I'm not your man. I told him what I heard from the morning guy." He said. "I've got only secondhand information."

Thomas bit down his lips. As much as he wanted to phone the morning guy, he understood time was of the essence. At least going by his premonitions, it was. He decided to settle for the available resources. "Alright, you're all I got." He said in two minds. "Lay it on me."

"White. Thirty-something. Early forties is possible too. Some people age better than others." He commented, before realizing to stick strictly to what was necessary. None of the three seemed very patient about it. "Brown hair. Looked a little huge, I heard."

"What's huge?"

"About twice the size you are..." He said. "... Mr.Lee." He added. That — to him — seemed a better choice than to say the guy was as big as himself. In actuality, he could recollect the morning guy saying *as big as you*. He didn't feel too good about it.

"Alright, alright." Lee took down the details in the pocket note he carried everywhere. "What about his name and phone number?"

"Well, sometime around, one of your guys tried calling him." He said, bending down to look at Theo sitting tightly behind. "He's not here with y'all, I think... The number's a fake." He said, to everyone's disappointment.

"Name?"

"That's probably a fake too." He laughed about it. "I don't know how he actually took down the name. I would have asked him again..." He said, full of himself. "... For his real name, of course." He continued, noticing the cops getting majorly impatient. "Jerome Biscuit. That's B-I-S-C-U-I-T. I'm not making this up." He laughed.

"Thanks, man, We'll take it from here." Thomas said, taking down the name with all the other details. "Run it in the database as soon as you get back to the precinct." He told Theo, handing him the sheet he tore off. Thomas started the car up again, ready to leave for other places. "So, we'll see you... I didn't get your name..."

[CENTRAL NARRATION ENDS]

CHAPTER XI

Collateral Damage

October 17, 2007

I broke out of all dizziness. The noise had sent a shiver through my spine, I could feel no pain for a long few seconds. For a moment, time seemed to freeze. With air gushing out of me uncontrollably, I couldn't utter a single proper word. I had jumped up to the ground without realizing it myself. Light in the head, I struggled to stand on two feet. Inside a closed car, with my only friend and boss bunged up in the backseat, and with airbags restricting free movement, I'd just heard a gunshot. A scream. And then, dead silence.

Front facing the smashed four-wheeler, I walked away, one foot back at a time. I could feel the weight of the night pressing down on me. Until I finally heard movement inside. I assumed one of them was alive at worst. The instinct to flee warred with curiosity. Continuing to move at an erratic pace, I was up for risking falling down on my face. Eyes wide open, mouth moving without words. I trembled. Because last I remembered, it was Daniel Jenson playing the dominant hand. I would have cried if not for a throbbing pain all over my face.

I could sense a pair of hands struggling to find the door handle. If I wasn't gonna turn back and take off, I was never gonna make it. I turned back. The hands seemed to clasp the handle after all. One goal in mind, and that was staying alive. Devon didn't seem to make it. I had to put my life before any grief, as is the right thing. I had to take whatever was the least likely direction a bullet could fly through. But I saw barren lands seemingly stretching through every which way. I didn't think. I ran.

The door opened. Amidst a misguided race to live long, I attempted to glimpse at the disappearing figures. They disappeared not because of distance, but because of watery eyes. A pair of hands in a black fabric was all I could make out. In all that chaos, it was a wonder I could recollect what color the fat Jenson wore. The trees, their leaves, the sand, and the streetlights: everything looked dark. Everything but white, of course. Too bright a color to get mixed up. Black looked darker. Images flashed before me. Images of Daniel Jenson moving around so my blood couldn't sully his white shirt.

And, that was it.

Had I simply turned around to rubberneck for a few seconds, the longer road could have well been avoided. I stopped dead in my tracks. It was Devon at the other end. I traced my path, wanting him to believe I was expecting this all along. He was in no position to question anything, though. Managing to get his fourth leg out of the vehicle, after the third, he gave himself up to the ground. His hands flailed in the air before flying back down with a thud. Sand erupted around him for a second. As I neared him with relief, it hit me. He had his right hand loosely wrapped around the gun. The gunshot. What had happened inside?

• • •

I was looking at a bloodbath. Almost ironic how he was so careful not to let me bleed as I wanted to. Sorry for him, helplessly lying in his own pool of blood. I couldn't bear to see so much graphic imagery nor could I look away, given that it probably was a sight I wouldn't get to see otherwise. "I killed him!" Devon cried from behind. He was as miserable if not more. His clothes were drenched in blood, he stank from head to toe. "He's dead." He added.

No, he wasn't. He moved around quite visibly. He was shot in his thighs. The bullet had pierced through his meaty legs, leaving significant holes along the way. It was quite a sight. Something I'd throw up on, if not for the crazy adrenaline rush I was recovering from. "Why the hell did you shoot him?" I asked, beginning to catch up to my senses. It was a question I had to ask as soon as I looked at Jenson lying half-dead.

"It had to be done!" He yelled, back on his foot again. He perspired an enormous amount. "Are you telling me you'd rather he kill me?" He hesitated to sneak a look inside the car. The blood dripping on the outside was just enough to push him away.

In the middle of nowhere, with unhuman sounds punctuating the silence, a twisted lamppost loomed over the rundown car. We were sure to get noticed if some good samaritan passed through. There was no way we were gonna drive around in that sad-looking piece of metal with a blood-covered body in the back. Jenson had to live. We had to save him. "He's not dead." I said slowly.

"What?"

"But he probably will be! Do something!" As I finished yelling, Devon pushed me hard. I tripped over, falling to the ground. He picked up the gun and emptied the bullets in a smooth fashion. Now, I lay between his legs, his shadow over mine. He stared at me, almost with disappointment.

"Fuck off, Cody." He mumbled, walking over to the other side. "You seriously didn't think I was gonna let him walk all over me. The entire day!" Louder and louder he grew, doing everything possible to get noticed. And get locked up. "The entire day, I was the fool. I was the joke. Jeff Walker laughed at me. Jenson did too. And, what about you? Look at him now!" He clenched his teeth, embodying the devil in all forms. "You know I am?" He shouted, crouching to the man dying of a gun wound. "I own your money!" He pushed an already fallen Jenson like it made things any different.

Silence followed. I waited for him to be done with his monologue. For him to come to understand the consequences of what had happened. As always, it took time for Devon to see things for what they were. He loosened up as he looked around the empty lands, completely in contrast to everything spread about the twenty feet around the car. I couldn't wait for longer than a minute, for with every passing second, the bossman neared death. As we all were, in a way. "Devon..." I began. "I'll come back with a medical kit."

"What are you talking about? Don't leave me with him."

"You brought this onto yourself." I argued. "It's your damned ego that's defeated you. Messed up your head. Poor judgment. You shot a man. He's dying-"

"Cody, stop."

"We were last seen with him. Say, we leave him here, Biscuit's gonna tell on us. The money's left with no owner. We're going to jail-"

"Cody, stop."

"I will not stop!" I could clench my teeth too, he had to know. I could get mad too, yell too. "Did you ever stop to think? You're in the middle of nowhere. But you just had to show me who you are. What are you gonna do now? Tell me. Tell me!"

"Let me think." Between when he asked to think, and when he found answers, Jenson was the one to bring it home. His phone, to be fair. The phone rang from inside. A muffled ringtone from his pant pockets. As grossed out as I was from all the flesh and blood, I was more in need of answers. In went my reluctant pair of hands, dodging all contact with his body, only for the phone it housed. As most unexpected, it was from someone who could be helpful. Though not the ideal candidate, someone was better than no one. Before answering the phone, it wasn't very clever of me to consult the red-faced Ledger.

"I'm gonna answer the phone." Despite it being a statement — not an ask for permission — Devon had to deny it since it wasn't his idea to throw around.

"I hope you're joking."

"I'm not joking." I replied, stepping further away from him. The phone was about to go off. I wasn't okay with being the one letting things slip away. So close were we to losing, anything seemed better than sitting around. I put my fingers on the lips, so as to not let Ledger spoil everything. I'd rather deal with Jeff than a dead Jenson. I answered the phone.

"Hello, Daniel. It's Jeff." I didn't say a word. Neither did Devon. "You, uh..." He continued. "... There's a document in the office. I'm in the Cleveland branch, actually." No words from my side. I could only assume he was nervous, for it wasn't every day Jeff spoke so many words without checking if the other end was listening. "Daniel, where are you?" He finally asked, before coming to conclude it probably wasn't Jenson.

Presumably on the verge of cutting away the phone call, Jeff Walker breathed loud enough for me to hear it over speakerphone. He would have ended it right there, if not for my indulgence. I hadn't a better choice. "Daniel can't come to the phone right now." Devon, finally, fell quiet without protest. What Jeff had to say was in his interest, after all.

"Who is this?" He asked, in a careful tone.

"Cody Mills." I responded, failing to find a reason to say otherwise.

"I'm sorry, who is this?" He repeated himself. Props to him, it could have well been a ploy. It was possible we'd set up a trap to catch him. It was possible Jenson was listening intently, holding his breath to find out if Jeff had anything to do with the name Cody Mills. That wasn't the case, sadly. Maybe, it was. Case in point, he *was* on speaker, and Daniel wasn't dead enough to go deaf.

"I said Daniel can't come to the phone. I'm not lying."

"Where are you?" He asked coyly, still not losing his cool. It was the best he could do, before going nuts all over. I wouldn't say I wasn't surprised.

"I don't know."

"Don't play games with me. I've had enough." And there he resumed his threats. I looked at Devon for his approval. Whatever was said and done, we were in this together. I shook my head, meaning I was ready to give in to temptations. I decided to spill the beans. It was the one last attempt at saving myself. Saving ourselves. Despite it not being understood by Devon Ledger. But again, when has he ever understood me?

"Jeff, we shot Jenson." I said, still not pinning the blame on the man directly responsible. "He's losing a lot of blood. We're somewhere between the office and my home. Take all the money..." I declared without deeper thought. "... Just-just don't let him die on us. We can't use this car now. It's totaled. We need you so bad." Honesty seemed to always work for me. With our backs against a concrete wall, why not go for it? Even if it's my worst enemy on the receiving end... At least, for the moment.

• • •

Just like that, Jeff wasn't gonna buy it, of course. I went on to admit that we shot him, giving away that we had a gun to ourselves. He asked for a guarantee that we weren't gonna shoot him. A guarantee on his life, which we couldn't give. Even worse, he asked for proof. If it's a photo of the gravely wounded bossman, I didn't have a camera phone. It wasn't a good enough reason though. Was it strange that he knew Jenson had a camera phone? I couldn't decide what was stranger: that or how he wasn't surprised for a millisecond that we'd shot the man. Perhaps, he didn't believe things he didn't get to see. Or perhaps, it was something else.

It had been thirty minutes since I'd made the distasteful video of Jenson holding on to life. Ledger — on the other side — wasn't kind enough to help me remove his pants. I had to listen to Daniel Jenson screaming and crying. "Save me-save me..." He murmured every now and again. I said sorry to keep him from crying. It didn't help. An alarming guilt rode over me. I tried making conversation. I asked him if there was a first aid kit in the car. I gave him water to drink. But the guilt went nowhere. Neither did the weeping. All while Devon Ledger smoked a cigarette till last.

Finally, Jeff's car pulled up at a distance near enough for us to know it was him. He flashed his headlights and honked at me. It was the sign we decided on. I walked towards him, raising my hands to the sky. I had to show I had nothing to hide. Ledger joined me hesitantly, now on his second cigarette. He groaned visibly as I threw the gun in the air, welcoming Jeff Walker in his own way. "If you don't help me with this, I'm never talking to you again." I told Devon instinctively. He put down his cigarette and walked along, a little more cautiously. For a second there, I couldn't believe it worked like a charm. "That's right." I added.

"So, we meet again." Jeff shouted across the air with one hand on his gun for safety. He could never be careful enough, he probably assumed. We didn't stop until we were ten feet apart. "Here's your medical kit." He said, throwing the bag at us. "Now, you honor your end of the deal."

"I don't know how to treat gun wounds." I said in the humblest tone known to me.

"That's your problem." He was keen on leaving. He'd only said yes because I offered him the keys to my house.

"Didn't you tell me you're very dangerous? That you've seen a lot of bad things. C'mon man, you're letting him die on us." I remarked, decidedly submissive.

"I'm not a doctor, you idiot. If you want him to live, take him to a doctor. Either that or be a bit smart and walk away." He said. I continued looking at him patiently. Ego had no place in this situation, and at the very least, I had to think clearly, if Devon couldn't. I stood by my words, abandoning all feelings of anger and resentment. He was the man. And, we needed the man. "How long has it been?" He eventually loosened up with a question.

"Since the wound? Since the-it's been around forty." Jeff stared in disbelief. He shook his head, a meek attempt at disapproval. I had to fight for approval again. "But, no. Hold on. I removed his pants. I-I tied it around the area, I did the basics. Last I checked, he was awake."

"I don't know man... He's not gonna make it. How many times do I have to tell you?"

"Come, take a look. That's all I ask!" As part of the deal, I handed him the keys to my apartment. Now that it was entirely his choice to make, a decision to be the bigger man would go well with his conceit. I was pretty confident nothing momentarily bad could come out of him having the keys to an apartment worth practically nothing over the money we owned. "Jenson's gonna know you came. You came and you did nothing. If you're so confident he wouldn't be alive to see the light of day, come on and take a look at him."

Upon a moment of consideration, he came to realize even the worst that could happen wouldn't look too bad for him. A second-long gaze followed by a pessimistic comment was all that he probably planned on. He walked up to the car, tucking his gun under the shirt. But he still was on his guard as I could confidently say from how he kicked our gun lying on the floor to his right with a self-approving smirk. He looked back to see if we followed him and did nothing particularly out of the ordinary.

We had already pushed the car a couple of feet across the lamppost. It looked better, at least from a psychological standpoint. Not that it made things any less noticeable. Jenson was lying crumpled up on the floor of the car with no light falling on him. I hadn't noticed that he'd made no noise for the last few minutes. Probably since I was occupied with getting Ledger back on track. It was *his* mess I was clearing up.

"Is he awake?" Jeff whispered. There was only one way to know. With whatever piece of clothing left over from covering up the entry wound, I had managed to wrap him up from head to toe. I couldn't bear to see him shaking with a straight face. It was only from his feet hanging limp out of the car, I could confirm he didn't switch places. The more Jeff advanced, the more Devon slowed down. The closeness crumbled apart so gradually for anybody to catch it over cursory glances.

"Tell me we can save him." I said naturally, as I stepped back a bit for Jeff to get a comfortable look at Daniel Jenson. Devon was only halfway. I couldn't give the signal yet. But one thing had to happen before the other for us to not look stupid. I reckoned Devon would eventually catch up. It was the better of the two options. Accompanying a concerned hiss, I began taking off the makeshift blanket from below.

"It doesn't look like-." Jeff began, confused at the neatly presented mishmash of red-orange dye in place of the horrifying mess he'd prepared himself to walk into. It didn't look like a gunshot, because it wasn't one.

"Didn't I tell you he's your man?" I had to show him the green light before it was too late. Jeff drifted back, as I got done with all the unwrapping. Thank goodness, Daniel had the gun, just ready to fire. The loading of the barrel had been done well in advance. Or so he said to Jeff Walker.

"The gun's loaded and ready to go off." Those were some first words of top quality for a half-hour preparation time. "Don't you take a step." The bossman warned him in the right tone. And with him, it was the second person of the day to take me for my word.

"What the fuck is going on?" Jeff screamed as we thought he would. Before he could reach out for the gun caressing his butt, Devon straightened him up with a second gun from behind. He couldn't believe his seemingly over-the-top nightmares weren't so over-the-top after all. "Daniel, what do you think you're doing?"

"What do you think *you're* doing?" He sent back the question. "You're my regional fucking manager. I don't understand a thing right now. I can't trust anyone."

"Daniel, listen to me. Listen to me. Whatever you decide, whomever you trust, don't trust these two. They're trying to turn it on me."

"Cut the bullshit, you criminal. I heard everything you had to say. You're after my money, they're just dummy tools. Dummy tools who ended up catching the mastermind for me."

"You've been brainwashed."

"How long has this been going on? How did you even know about the vault? About the money..." Daniel pulled himself up, beginning to close in on his regional manager. "... Or did you only join the company to steal from me?"

"Daniel, listen to yourself. I have been working for J.J. Designers for thirteen years. Working for you for 13 years. Do you trust these two lowlives more than you trust me?"

"At the moment, yes." He said, looking at me with suppressed anger. We had crashed his car but got away with it, only by dropping Jeff's name. When he got to know that his regional manager had gone behind his back, Jenson fantastically played along, pretending to have suffered a gunshot. I should have offered him for grabs before the unneeded swerve of the car."They're cheap filth. I slapped him around for ten minutes." Daniel pointed to me. "He started crying like a girl. Gave himself up, and then the entire story came along."

"A story full of lies!" He yelled, curling his fists to throw a punch at me. He didn't expect to see me unfazed. Jenson sniggered and raised the revolver up to his face. He shook his head, taken down by a gut-wrenching feeling of betrayal. Laughing to himself, he smashed the gun against his own head once and twice. More than anyone, he hated himself for being so blind. "You're making a mistake." Walker added.

"Are you going to die right here? Or, are you going to look alive and give up the truth? Talk about everything that went behind your little operation. Is there anyone else you're not telling me about?"

The regional manager didn't succumb to his boss or his tactics. His sense of time was so bad he thought it to be a time to revisit sarcasm. "I've never seen a bigger idiot. How the hell did they convince you that crashing your expensive car was the only way to the truth?" After which, he was ballsy enough to throw a laugh at his face. Jenson smacked his gun at Jeff's face. "Aagh!" He screamed, holding his nose in intense pain.

"I figured I could drive your car once I shoot you down." He smiled again, thinking to himself he'd won the argument rightfully.

"Come to think of it, all of this worked only because you had two guns with you." Devon indulged with a smile. Jenson nodded slowly. We were on his team not because he trusted us. But because he hated Jeff more than he hated us. It's not as if he had anyone to turn to about bringing home his black money. Given the circumstances, a nod was the best he could do. Devon could have stayed mute for the better.

Jenson reached into Jeff's pocket for the keys to his ride. "You. Drive the car to your home." He waved at me. "When I see the money, I'll think about letting you off the hook." He pushed around Jeff, possibly towards his car. But before we moved, we were forgetting something.

"Hey, Mr.Jenson." I said. "Before anything, I think we should do something about your car over there." I suggested politely. With his immediate approval, we got to work.

CHAPTER XII

Closer Than Ever

[CENTRAL NARRATION PLAYS]

Officer Thomas Lee got out of the police van right outside the convenience store. What started out with a needlessly overcrowded pack of five police officers now came down to an unpopulated team with Thomas and Justin to spare. Theo was let go halfway, partly thanks to the intolerable bulk of things he tried getting the group to commentate on. Mainly, since they would rather exert themselves than deploy the night-shifters to come up with delicate information. There were more than a few things they were waiting for Theo to dial back about.

Justin carefully grabbed the two-month-old bill and skimmed over the area for any and all security cameras. The store occupied the ground floor of the three-storeyed building also home to a make-up parlor above and a printing press further above. Their mascot — a thoughtful redesign of the conventional shopping cart — hung over the bright yellow signboard: the setting, strikingly dissimilar from all the tasteless commercial quarters above and aside.

A multitude of surveillance systems had been inching along the highway for longer than ten miles only to fall short a couple of blocks, losing to a sharp right into the street housing the departmental store. For a street no stranger to passing cars past sunset, it would have been fruitless to course through hours of highway footage looking for a drop in the ocean. The only relevant place of interest was the camera staring down the automatic doorway from above the cardboard mascot.

With everything visible to the naked eye a subject to his suspicion, Thomas ingressed the building wearing an unhealthily overconfident expression. He couldn't help it though, for it had forever been his resting face in the interrogation room. Justin followed him, picking up the pocket note his partner had left behind. Despite an unbeatable curiosity to flip through the pages and gauge his competence, Justin handed the notebook first thing as they locked eyes. He'd rather live life happily telling himself that they aren't the same people.

The store opened to an immediate wall blocking one side, with a billing counter at the far end. The entire shopping section spread about on the opposite side for about a generous thirty feet. With neatly organized shelves and straightforward aisles, the minimally-lit quarters didn't assumably welcome too many consumers. A grown woman, of about forty-five, jumped up from her plastic chair on seeing a customer. It wasn't long until Thomas wiped off her smile with a wave of his badge. Deceptively grand from the outside, the rather simple interior took Thomas by surprise. The air was a notch too sadder than he'd have asked for.

He leaned into Justin to whisper. "Go check out the top floors." As Justin walked away from him with pace, Thomas snapped his fingers for attention. The woman, alarmed on one hand, and confused on the other, fidgeted with her pen. She waited for Thomas to talk before allowing herself to. She deemed it wise to be a little too careful with cops in the night. "Hey there, how you doing?" Thomas began.

"Yeah..." She hesitated. "... I'm okay." So she declared, as her eyes constantly bounced off the gun in the holster and the badge in his hand. "How can I help you?"

"How many security cameras do you have around?" He questioned.

"Is there a problem?" Thomas clicked his tongue; a tired sigh followed. It was commonplace for him to try and cut straight to the chase before all formalities. It's a lucky day when the person offers to blurt out all the answers with nothing in return. He'll know a pushover when he sees one. Formalities followed if need be. But when there were questions from the other end right from the beginning, it was nature's way of telling him he didn't have it easy. He subtly pursed his lips, readying a better maneuver. "Five cameras. Six, but one doesn't work." She gave in.

His face turned around in no time. He might have even cracked a smile. He got himself together and thanked his Gods. "Right." His tone, authoritative as ordinary. "Which one doesn't work?" He asked, hoping it wasn't the one out front. She pointed her fingers, fortunately, to a corner that didn't need cameras in any case. Before she repeated herself making everybody's mood unpleasant, Thomas reckoned it to be the time for info-dumps.

"We're out after a violent man. He broke out of prison this morning and we think your security cameras could help us find him."

"Sure." She immediately came forward. "What do you need?"

"Do you still have six-week-old footage?" By a show of hands, she politely asked him to hold on patiently before hot-footing to the backroom. The inconspicuous door, identical in look and color to the walls it was sandwiched between, looked effortlessly natural — Thomas didn't think one possibly existed until she disappeared into it. Fighting the urge to lean into her private space around the billing counter, Thomas attempted to collect his thoughts from all the investigatory exercises so far. And, there came out the pocket note.

Could he spot the runner from the video footage, it was already a sign they were getting closer than ever. If there was any luck lurking behind, it was possible he could also single out the vehicle he used back then. Given that nobody had all the time to go through every minute of the day and find out if, at all, he visited the store more than once, Thomas had to come up with a better way to exploit such valuable physical evidence. He restricted himself from going too far and beyond though. What if, God forbid, they'd already taped over the old footage?

Justin didn't return. Neither did the lady. Since she'd put him in charge without explicitly saying so, it wouldn't be fair to move away. He held on to his patience. A minute passed. Thomas drove himself to decide it was high time he checked in on the rookie. He pulled out his phone and dialed him up.

"Hey, Theo!" He exclaimed, relieved as the rookie swiftly answered. He couldn't himself understand where the relief stemmed from. It wasn't as though his life was at risk inside a police precinct.

"Thomas, I was hoping you'd call." He could have never guessed he'd ever jump up and down hearing Theo say those words. But from how he sounded, Thomas made up his mind that good news waited. No one could say otherwise.

"Tell me you have good news."

"Good news, I think so. Yes?" He said, sounding half-sure.

Justin walked in that very moment, shaking his head along the way. He knew Thomas inside out, he just had to make sure the guy didn't jump to early conclusions. Before he could introduce words for further clarification, Thomas interjected with words of his own. He seemed to welcome Justin with a great deal of excitement letting him assume Thomas had already jumped to conclusions. Justin began to warn Thomas not to get too crazy over his pointless trip up the stairway. Until he came to realize he was the one jumping to premature conclusions. "Theo's on the phone." He had since heard him say.

"What?" The rookie asked from the other line, reasonably baffled over the ruckus he could only hear, not see. "Thomas, are you there?"

"Yeah, I'm here. Justin's here too." He answered Theo. "He's got some news." He then told Justin, without making it clear who's got what — having forgotten Theo wasn't physically present.

"What's up, Justin?" Theo began.

"Hey, what's up man?" A classic exchange of meaningless niceties. Or, so he assumed.

"So, what's the news?" Theo asked.

"What's the news, I was gonna ask you that." Justin replied.

"Yeah, but... You have news?"

"What news?"

"Thomas told."

"Thomas told what?"

"That you got news."

"When?"

"Just right now. Seconds ago. You heard him!" The rookie raged.

"I don't understand..." Justin dragged. Just as he was beginning to think Thomas probably talked about him behind his back, Thomas chose to interrupt, thankfully with the answer to all the confusion. Before Justin could further misinterpret, and before Theo could hang up on the lot, Thomas rose to the occasion.

"Guys, guys! Theo, I told Justin you have a story to share. You thought I was talking to you... about Justin. In actuality, I was talking to Justin about you. Didn't strike me we were miles apart. Miscommunication. It happens." He claimed. "Move on." He yelled over the phone animatedly before catching a look to his side.

The shopkeeper had been listening for who knew how long. From the funny look on her face — he'd assumed — quite a bit. "You'll have to excuse us for a moment." He quickly declared, power walking toward the entrance. Justin followed.

• • •

Outside the store wasn't half as silent as inside. But on any given day, they'd take the buzzing traffic over discomforting looks from the jaded woman. Thomas made the phone call again, not as certain he'd pick up this time. But, as rookies do when the big men come calling, Theo answered the phone quicker than earlier, with no recollection of the past. "Hello..." He even went on to initiate.

"Theo, sorry about that." Thomas said. "*You* have something to tell me. And *we* would like to hear. Now that that's cleared up, can you go ahead?"

"Yes, Thomas." He chuckled perfunctorily. "I ran the name Jerome Biscuit in the system. We have no records relating to that name."

"Doesn't sound like good news to me." He cut him off.

"But, I have something else." The two policemen looked at each other, nodding their heads with interest. "I could find only one Jerome Biscuit on the internet. Lucky for us, it's a very weird name."

He dragged the delivery on purpose. Though not completely on board with the approach, they had to hold their horses to get to the truth. "Guess what, he's one of the managers at a company that goes by the name J.J.Designers."

"Wow. Solid work, good man." Justin commented.

"No, no. It doesn't end there. J.J.Designers, this company, is just about two miles from where you are right now."

"Are you serious?" Thomas had to ask, of course.

"Yeah, but..." He dragged. But only now, not for a very good reason. "There's a catch. This guy's over fifty and if the pictures are real, he looks too old to pull off a thirty-year-old."

"If I'm allowed to interrupt..." Justin chimed in, being a gentleman about asking the rookie for permission to talk. "... I thought about it. From the mug shots, it's pretty clear Keith's got black hair. And this guy, Biscuit, he's got, what, gray hair, I guess?" Theo confirmed. "I mean, logically speaking, Keith didn't probably dye his hair on his way out of prison. If the Biscuit man is still gray-haired, we can safely say the guy whom the security guard identified was, all in all, a completely different individual."

"Where are you going with this?" Lee interrupted.

"Hold on, you're throwing me off the track. I'm making it up as we speak." Justin asserted. "I don't think I would randomly throw around a name this strange unless I somehow slipped up. Maybe, the suspect we're looking at, he's working for or with Keith Warren. He's heard the name Biscuit somewhere quite recently, and he was as amazed as we were upon hearing the name. Reasonable, yeah?" He checked to see if he didn't lose them.

"Maybe, he didn't think he would need to give out a name and a phone number and fucked it up when he was put on the spot. Maybe he knew Jerome Biscuit already. Or maybe, he has something to do with that name. Now, pay attention, it's possible Biscuit knows shit. But, you know what? It's also very possible he doesn't even know this guy exists. Either way, I think J.J.Designers is worth investigating."

“That’s what I would assume too, yeah.” Thomas said. With merely a couple of words, the detective stole credit for what was a very thoughtful conjecture.

“Man, that’s genius!” Theo exclaimed.

“Thank you.” He said, only to follow it up with added genius. “If it’s not too late, I think we should go talk to Jerome Biscuit. Ask him a few questions, and see if he’s weird about it. It’s only a two-mile drive, Theo says.”

“Theo...” Thomas interjected. “... where exactly did Keith get picked up?”

“I don’t know.” He immediately replied. “I thought you asked Fletcher to get on that.”

“Is Fletcher with you now?”

“No...” He said innocently.

“So, who’s doing his job?”

“I’ll get back to you.” Theo submitted. Thomas hung up the phone sharply. With an entirely new person now in the picture, they had to re-discuss strategies. All while being two heads short and constantly on the run. Justin walked away and toward the police van.

“Think I’ll talk to Theo and go check out J.J.Designers.” He said.

“Justin, wait,” said Thomas. “First things first, we have some video footage to look at.”

• • •

The shopkeeper rifled through a plastic box full of hard drives. Cameras 3 through 6 covered all the aisles and walkways. It was the second one at the bill counter the coppers were banking on. The woman fished out five hard drives from the previous month. Having laid them out in some fashion, she gaped at the batch, thinking she could bring it down to the one or two pertaining to the time and day in question.

From the detective’s perspective, whatever information coming out of her was directly tied to how important she was. A penniless worker could lie without a worry — it’s not every day she has two policemen on their toes for her to speak up. "Are you the owner?" Thomas asked, nonchalant in his head, yet struggling to lose authority on the outside.

She adjusted her glasses, shooting an ugly look for whatever reason. "Yes. I own the place."

"How often do you get customers?" He asked judgmentally.

"Not often." She remarked with a petty undertone.

"A little too grand for no customers." He casually suggested, looking the other way.

She closed in on the hard drives, keeping two from the pile aside with a thud. Not wanting to lose the conversation, she effectively moved on to better topics. "So, do you wanna take a look or what?"

Justin wandered to her side of the table before Thomas could craft a fitting response. Now, it was only a waiting game until he realized catching Keith was the order of the day. The woman loaded up the hours and hours of footage on her square screen computer. So slow was the machine's operational speed, everyone but the lady toyed with the idea of grabbing a smoke meanwhile. But she didn't move an inch, for it could have well been the only computer she'd ever got her hands on. Eventually, Thomas circled around the table.

"We're almost there." She announced, after an eternity's time had easily passed. "Give me the bill." Justin had somehow reached a conclusion the impending stopover at J.J.Designers wasn't as big a priority anymore. "There you go, camera 2." She signaled with a sigh of relief.

Justin produced a folded paper from his pocket, handing Thomas the front-faced photograph of the runner. He shook his head as though it had already come to be a face he wouldn't forget anytime soon. Fair enough, for it was the first time he was out after a potentially dangerous man. Although, one couldn't easily say so because of how naturally he'd fooled himself to assume the disposition of a veteran, tired of catching psychopaths all day — a rather deliberate effort.

"Run it through to quarter past midnight." He said. The footage buffered, delaying the output to possibly induce a fatal adrenaline rush. Theo called at exactly the wrongest moment. Justin — on the prowl for a reason to look away — snatched the phone from Thomas before he could bang the phone against the table. As he bailed out on the group choosing Theo over crucial video evidence, the footage played out from 12:15 AM.

Thomas clutched onto his pocket note. Two minutes had already passed with no one in the range but the shopkeeper. And then came someone. It wasn't Keith Warren. Thomas moved closer to the screen. White, check. Thirty-something, check. Huge, check. His smile grew noticeably wider. It wasn't Keith Warren, but probably as good as him was his partner. "Justin, my phone!" He yelled across the air. "Come, look here. Take a photo of this, Justin!" Even louder. In no universe did the man look like a gray-haired manager. If Thomas wasn't half-blind, the man matched the security's description guard impeccably.

Justin came running. "Thomas, there's news from Theo."

"Come over here." Thomas called. Clear as day, the video was about the suspect buying instant noodles in the dead of night. Thomas couldn't be more confident when he declared it was impossible for two to feed on one pack of cheap cup noodles. While still standing by his earlier supposition, he had to check the entrance footage for the sake of police work. "Load up the footage from camera 1." He ordered, without thinking much of it.

The lady eyeballed the policemen, groaning viciously. "What about this one? That'll take me even longer."

"Thomas, listen to me." Justin interrupted her mercilessly. "Six weeks ago, Keith was picked up just a *few blocks* away from J.J.Designers." He warned in a restrained voice. It was an obvious sign asking him to step out and away from the civilian he was practically leaning on. Thomas fell silent. "We're so close. The more you put this off, the more you're risking it." Justin warned.

The footage buffered again. A red sedan appeared in dim light. Thomas held back on an active response to Justin, shushing him with a flap of his hand. It was the same night and the same time. The camera above the name board provided a much wider range of vision than anticipated. Thomas leaned in to confirm it was the same red sedan they had ripped apart. "You told me it's gonna take you even longer."

"Well, it didn't." The salty woman remarked.

"Thomas, give me the car keys." Justin slowly raised his voice. The man alighting from the car — as predetermined— was Keith's supposed partner, despite there being no evidence to prove for or against. Throwing the cigarette to the ground, the man was seen checking his shirt and pants for money enough to buy some food for the night. On the second camera, he was seen entering the store at 12:18 a.m. Between when he entered and exited the convenience store, he wasn't seen with his car keys. Thomas..." Justin indulged.

"Will you give me a minute?" He gnarled, pointing to the computer. The car left unparked, occupying half the lane, the keys still probably in the ignition, everything pointed towards a common conclusion. As the suspect returned, he raised the cup noodles in the air to answer someone within the tinted windows. The door flew open. Caucasian, 32, black hair, and a pretentious goatee.

"I've seen this man." The lady came back to life. Thomas leaned in, only an inch between his eyes and the screen.

"We got him." Thomas mumbled. A developing grin enveloped his face. He couldn't stop smiling. "We got him!" He celebrated to himself. It was the man himself, Keith Warren. Justin allowed himself to crack a smile. He acknowledged his partner. Thomas was on to something, after all.

"I said I've seen this man!" The shopkeeper repeated with more intensity. Thomas looked at her, still stuck in a celebratory mood. "Today. I saw him today."

"What?"

"Do you not hear me? He came to my store today. He came here!" The cops shared glances, they weren't gonna believe her without doubts. "Do you want me to get you today's footage?"

"How long has it been?" Thomas questioned.

"I don't know, a couple of hours." Justin found the car keys inside Lee's pockets. He was in no mood to wait, no matter what the woman had to say.

"Thomas, I'm leaving."

"Justin..." He tried. "Justin!" He had to stop and turn around. At least to ask Thomas why he had to scream at the top of his lungs. A good detective should know Justin was trying to do the right thing. It might well be true, but why would a right-minded Thomas let someone else take charge? He considered being the bigger man. Frankly though, he knew he wasn't cut out for that. "Give me the keys, I'll go."

"But..." He hesitated, for it had been him forever wanting to drop by J.J.Designers.

"Someone should go, I'll go. You stay back, talk to her, take down details." He plucked the keys off his partner's hands and stormed out before he could retaliate. Whatever the time and day, Thomas just *had* to be the man to bring it home.

[CENTRAL NARRATION ENDS]

CHAPTER XIII

Stranger Danger

October 17, 2007

We had inhabited Jeff Walker's sumptuous car without his approval. I was done with chauffeuring around everybody who ever owned a firearm. First things first, I had to find a way to get myself out of it. It was all I thought about until I remembered we were all driving to my home. With not one, but two guns in his hand, Daniel Jenson was twice as dangerous. On seeing me penniless, there shouldn't be too many options for Jenson but to shoot me on the spot. Was I gonna come clean, an hour ago was about the right time to do so.

Jeff — on the backseat alongside Jenson — was a bloody mess from catching a strike from the revolver. Lucky for him, he ended up using the medical kits he'd bought with his own money. Devon, as usual, had lapsed back into monk mode from the moment he was thrown into the front seat. I comfortably imagined he was freaking out as well. Just not explicitly. "How much longer?" Jenson asked.

"We're almost there. Five minutes." For all the injuries I had sustained that night, I was nowhere near Jeff and his unparalleled take on physical pain. He whimpered now and then, blowing his nose hard the rest of the time. So much cotton he had used up for some reason, I was expecting Jenson — now with two guns to whack his staff, not one — to go off at any moment giving Jeff more reason to tear apart the rest of the cotton roll. To prove me wrong, he remained as calm as Daniel Jenson was publicly known to be.

For once I wasn't on the receiving end, and all that drama had hurt my ability to ideate. I would have much rather gone home with a cast and a black eye in exchange for an idea to get me out alive. Jenson had gotten lost elsewhere as it had been three minutes since he made any fuss and two minutes since he looked away from the window. Looking to crack my arms while still on the steering wheel, I casually bent aside to unintentionally knock off my partner nodding away. My biggest fear being that the bossman might slip back to reality right as I make my move.

But he didn't. Neither did Devon Ledger. I was out here worrying that we were nearing the end. All I yearned for was for Devon to so much acknowledge that we were on our way to becoming dead meat. And maybe also telepathically catch my plan to swerve the vehicle toward a water hydrant this time around. I was beginning to understand why he wouldn't look at me. Nobody was up for a second car accident. Frankly, I could still hear a long, ringing noise at the back of my head.

Against my will, I had driven myself to face death. We reached my apartment. The entrance left ajar was probably wide enough for us to pass through. I honked, hoping someone would take it for a desperate cry for help. "What the hell are you doing?" Jenson yelled restrictively.

"The gates." I said slowly.

"Won't he get down and push it open?" Saying so, he smacked Devon's head lightly. The security guard came trudging from the dark. It wasn't Jonathan. Breaking the short-lasted dormancy, Jenson gripped his revolver and pushed Jeff Walker to the floor. It was safe for nobody to see a bleeding man and a revolver.

The security guard opened the gates for us to enter. I suppose he did recognize me from somewhere. It wouldn't have mattered anyway. He never really took it upon himself to allow or deny entry. Had it been Jonathan in his place, had he somehow taken a gander at Jeff Walker being suffocated behind, he'd have recognized something was off. His replacement — on the other hand — might as well hold a sign saying the belly doesn't let him walk.

I drove the car past the parking lot, towards one of the darkest corners of the enclosure. At least from seeing me park vehicles in the oddest of spots, if only someone picked up the hint. "Wipe it off." Jenson threw his handkerchief at Jeff. He really *did* bring a handkerchief in one pocket and a gun in the other. We got out of the car and slowly advanced to the building. Daniel Jenson made sure to feed us with every little detail.

It was only on getting to the third floor I wished for Jonathan to magically burst into sight. I wished for Devon to take the bullet. I wished for myself to hold a gun. I wished for us to go back in time and do things differently.

For one thing, Jonathan would have told me about a guy looking like a jail convict coming to visit me. The last thing I wanted was for Keith Warren to come after me. Whatever the fuck happened to his prison time.

Lost Connections

CHAPTER XIV

Bad Old Days

A new life meant new beginnings. Following a near-death experience, the group had come to a consensus: No more violent crimes. They stood over the river in Saginaw, holding a heavy cardboard box. They had stacked it up with guns, papers, and all kinds of memorabilia relating to their criminal past. The first step in the moving-on process was to destroy any evidence from the past. "Don't dump it. Burn it," said Keith Warren.

Going from being full-blown hitmen to nobodies doesn't happen overnight. Particularly, with all the weight of the past slowing you down. The best they could do was become whole different people. At least, from the outside.

Unsurprisingly, the first thing that struck their heads was to move all the way to the west. But, time and money didn't give them a helping hand. It wasn't the first time the cops took their people out. But, this was the biggest yet. Nobody remained — at least, nobody brave enough to go out again.

The only sensible idea came through Keith. "My parents live in Cleveland." He'd waited for minutes banking on the rest to come up with a better idea — something that didn't involve his mum and dad. When all plans were exhausted, he had to give himself up for good. "I didn't wanna say it." He followed it with deeply personal remarks. "And I can't imagine how ugly it's gonna be when I talk to my mum after three years and *I've killed people* are gonna be my first words."

"If that's how you're gonna open your conversation, then yeah." The old man laughed through his remaining teeth. Nobody paid him any attention. A little too bold, coming from a man who can barely walk for a mile. If not for how he fell at their legs and wept until they agreed, he wouldn't be standing there. Only had he right away revealed he had a lot of money, they would have heartily welcomed him.

The poor guy had imagined money was never gonna be a problem. Given that they'd spent years sticking with criminals, they should be rolling in money. They *should* be, except they weren't. As part of the cleaning-out operation, the cops had also gobbled up whatever was left. Without a penny in their pockets, they'd been practically waiting for an old-timer with savings to join their team. Moving towns isn't a cheap affair. Now is when they needed money more than anything.

• • •

It hadn't been a week, and more than half his money had been spent. To deplete the wealth he'd saved up for years didn't take seven days. They had convinced him it was all important to their mission — some mission they didn't know half about. Grateful as he was to finally be a part of something, he'd given them his blessings to make him go broke. They had all moved to Cleveland, renting different houses in all corners of the city. And just like that, they'd spent the rest of the cash.

The first week took its toll on them. Having gotten used to getting up every morning and reaching for the gun, it seemed strange to not own a gun for the first time in a while. They weren't all for having a normal life. But, they'd seen enough nightmares to know they wouldn't hold a gun again. Keith Warren was especially hellbent on this: he wasn't gonna spill blood with his mother in the city at any cost.

Since moving westward was part of the grander scheme of things, they had to make the most out of this gestation period. As they had predicted, it hadn't been a hundred hours before they began rethinking these decisions. They met every day to counsel one another and collectively make sure no one fell back into old ways. They were jobless and idle, but there never was a day they didn't meet for coffee and cigarettes.

The old man happily hosted them every evening. They all listened to him talk about gawking at a woman down the street — all the poor man wanted was her necklace. More often than not, they had to restrain him from going further. He didn't know boundaries, and certainly couldn't say how much sharing is too much sharing. For the first twenty-odd days, they had successfully gotten the better of their kleptomaniacal self. Until Keith decided not to show up for a change.

Days after days, Keith wasn't seen outside. They'd only moved to Cleveland for him. He'd promised he could take care of them if things went south. Hoping he'd come back with money, they waited. They waited for twelve days. Their group meetings were on their way to becoming redundant. The thought of already losing out a member had consumed their heads. The old man began plotting to steal what looked like a diamond necklace. Nobody was in the right mind to stop him from fantasizing.

Enough is enough, they decided. The one thing Keith had always advised them against was to even think about dropping by his parents' place. He had discreetly crafted an elaborate ruse to talk his parents into giving him money. He'd always space out between conversations like something troubled him from within. They could tell he had something up his sleeve. But when he went missing for twelve days, they had to throw the rulebook out the window. Their first thought was something along the lines of meeting with his parents.

They jumped into the rented black Chrysler and set off to where they were the most unwelcome. Had they sat another twelve days straight, they would have reconsidered moving back to Michigan. No way in hell did they own enough green to make it through another month. They'd rather fall dead than take up a job in Cleveland. Their first step towards falling dead was meeting Keith's parents behind his back.

"Mrs.Claude." They told the security guard. Unlucky for him, Keith somehow dropped her name in the passing. They all remembered her name for some reason and it paid off. As they were guided to the apartment, they looked at one another in fear. Keith might have perchance never visited his parents. A truck might have run over him. Or, worse, the gang might have got to him. Although, when they left town, there *was* no gang to speak of.

Before the old man's legs grew sore, they knocked on the door. The door moved backwards. Good for them, maybe bad: Keith was on the other side. His eyes bulged. His lips curved to a grimace. He looked twice to confirm if they had really brought the old man along. "Go away!" He whispered, chasing the three away.

"Where the hell did you go for twelve days?" Devon couldn't resist.

"Keith, who's at the door?" A masculine voice came from behind. He was forced to respond. Saying nobody would still probably land him in trouble. He contemplated before turning to answer. Keith slipped a bit as the door creaked wide open. It was the impatient Mrs.Claude pulling the door from behind.

"Who the hell are you lot?" She crassly asked.

"We..." They hesitated.

"Uh, they're old friends. I'll meet them some other time. It's no big deal." The three others attempted to acquiesce as the woman showed them she couldn't be taken for a fool.

"You're telling me this old gentleman is your old friend?" Before the oldster could nod his head, they were half inside. Keith could have at least said they were strangers. They took a seat in the middle of the room for the parents to grill them with queries from all sides.

"How do you know Keith?" His father posed a question to everyone in common.

"Just from the old days." Cody replied quickly.

"Doing what exactly?" As Keith tried to offer help with answers that could blend into his story, his father shut him up. He stayed still to hear what the guests had to say.

"Just, you know... Things. We're from Saginaw."

"But he told us he had no friends there."

"Mom..." Keith interrupted.

"Will you let them talk?" His dad asked dominantly, nicely following it up with a quirky smile. "You're acting like you don't want us to hear them talk." After that, he could interject no more.

It was his motive to evade suspicions, not invite them. But it was enough time for Cody to craft a safe response.

"I thought we were your friends." He directed it to Keith. "I don't wanna be somewhere I'm not welcome."

"Oh, stop that." She said. "I'm not naive." She continued, turning to the old man for some reason. "Your son shows up after so many years. He expects nothing. He tells you he's rented out a place on Sixth Avenue. Didn't bother to ask you beforehand. What would you think of him?" His company shook their heads in unison. It was as much as they could do without physically shutting him up. They held their breaths to see how he'd respond.

"What are you suggesting?" It was Devon butting in to take on her questions. Her son gritted his teeth, fuming on the side. Devon chose not to notice him. She was taken aback for a second, shifting her eyes across the room.

"My son doesn't want me to know something..." Claude speculated. "... I think." She corrected herself. "And, you people could help me out here, I believe." They needed time to process her since they'd only expected problems to come from Keith himself. It was as natural for them to zone out as it was for Keith to lose himself to paranoia. Between when they stopped to think and considered answering, her son decided to come clean.

"I've killed people." He decided it would rather be him than someone else. Though, he could have trusted his partners to come up with something that wasn't the truth. He shuddered involuntarily. He clenched his fists but it didn't help. His nerves had wronged him. He'd rushed it. Now, he had to deal with the aftermath before three other men who were not family. He pushed his tears back.

"*We* have killed people." The senior citizen came forward to give the crying man a supportive hand. The father rose from his chair, and then the mother. The mess that followed was indescribable.

It took the four guys longer than a day's time to convince the parents not to go to the police. It took Keith Warren a week more to persuade his mother to cover for him if need be. She had to go from being a stickler for rules to *this*, for the sake of her son. They readied her with a fabricated account of the past. She didn't stoop to their level until they assured her that nine times out of ten, the police had no business looking for Keith Warren in Cleveland.

His dad, though, decided it was better for him to stay out of everything. He left his wife high and dry, taking an impromptu vacation for an umpteen number of days. Mrs.Claude hated herself for raising a failure for a son. She contained so much melancholy she could cry on cue.

• • •

Though not as normal, things went back to the way they were. Keith was living hell and he had no one to take it out on. He attended no more group discussions. Because he had to drop off his mother's hard-earned money at their places, he couldn't cut off ties with them just yet. Slowly but surely, the group meetings derailed from their original ideas; they no longer talked about fighting the urge to go back in time.

A month had passed. Keith showed up for the group meeting for a change. He had different plans though. As Cody talked at length about his recurring nightmares, Keith cut him short. "Look. Let me be straight." He said, leaning forward. "It's been a month. I can't keep giving you money for free. Pack your things and move to the west." He declared. "I'll stay with my mum. Obviously."

"Woah, woah. What happened to us moving to the west together?" Keith paused to stare at Cody in disbelief.

"Ask yourself that. Should have used your brain a little before showing up at my house." He tossed the week's finances onto the table and stormed out. Needless to say, they were collectively mad at themselves for not standing up to Keith.

"Why the hell should I leave Cleveland if he's gonna stay?" Devon raised his voice.

"Now that he's out of the way, what's the plan?" The old man whispered. Cody flung a notebook to him.

“Everything about J.J.Designers.” Cody announced. “I’ve got myself an interview.”

“Fuck, you made a whole notebook, did you?”

“I told you I was serious.”

“Do we tell Keith about it?” They exchanged wry smiles, knowing damn well what the right answer was. Cody leaned back, seeming to consider it for a second.

“I don’t think so.” He grinned sarcastically. “How about you get an interview too?” He asked Devon. “It’s not legal money, remember? The place is a shithole. No proper security. Half the cameras don’t work.”

“That’s not the point.” Devon countered. “How on God’s green earth do you plan to find out where the cash is stored? If the cash is stored? You want me to take a job because you said so.” He pettily flipped open the notebook.

“Do you have a better solution?” The old man asked. They had come so far without blood money that it was shameful they were about to return to square one. They could always tell they would have to come back to it sometime or the other. But, no one imagined orchestrating a crime of this degree this soon. Except this time, they didn’t work under anyone reaping most of the profit. “It’s black money. They can’t go to the police,” said the old-timer.

Cody Mills and Devon Ledger joined the company of J.J.Designers. They worked round the clock to devise the perfect strategy. When they pelted rocks at cameras and nobody cared, they understood this was the time to shine. The old man kept to his easy chair, going about the desk duty. Neither could they cut him off nor could they take him along.

When he finally retired to Richard Medical Centre without choice, he had to temporarily adopt the surname Mills, becoming Michael Mills. As part of the story, Michael became the uncle Cody never had. But when push did come to shove, Cody had to cut out Michael from the picture.

CHAPTER XV

Off The Mark

Officer Thomas Lee received calls all around from Justin to Theodore before he could reach the premises of J.J.Designers. The detectives back in the precinct had found out whom the red sedan belonged to. From what Thomas heard over the phone, it fit the description perfectly. Now armed with the sidekick's name and face, he was positive Keith would fall down soon enough. Caleb Davidson, it wasn't a name Thomas was gonna remember for long though.

Justin returned with good news too. From how they began to how things stood, the latter half of the day had been smoother by leaps and bounds. When the old store owner announced she'd seen Keith again that very day — a news ideally welcoming relentless festivities — Thomas had to play it down particularly since Justin was hellbent on abandoning him. It was only upon mindful remembrance he allowed himself to punch down the steering wheel in delight.

Once Justin double-checked her words with camera footage, he considered looking further into it before realizing that a three-hour-old footage wasn't as important. Hell, one could cross borders in a matter of three hours. But what intrigued the detectives was the purchase he'd made: a huge roll of cotton and antiseptics. Assuming that he'd hurt himself running through thorny bushes and poison ivy for hours, Thomas closed in on all the different places he could go from there. Yet, he couldn't help but loiter back to one little detail he could base nothing on: The Michigan Bandits.

After parking his car in one of the tons of unoccupied parking spaces around the compound, Thomas had the rookie on the phone. "Theo, there's one more thing." He went, first thing on the phone. They'd had over ten phone conversations that very day, there wasn't a need to exchange pleasantries. "Do you remember the

Michigan bandits?"

"I remember. You were telling us something."

"We're closing in on that bastard from every corner. There's that one piece of information we didn't look into." Thomas asserted. "If there's nothing else on your table, get on that right away. I'm walking into J.J.Designers, as we speak."

"Right." He replied. "Be careful, Thomas."

• • •

His first impression from looking at the quarters wasn't interesting enough to make it into his pocket note. However, he did find it a peculiar choice to build an office between a cluster of noisy textile mills. From the narrow pathway leading up to the office to the constant running of heavy machinery from afar: the lonely atmosphere appeared neither safe enough nor dangerous enough. Just the right combination for an outlaw to seek refuge, Thomas told himself.

Thomas prepared to encounter any nuisance from the guards with the mundane wave of his badge, only to locate the one security guard in his booth going about his own business. At around 8 p.m., he walked past the unguarded doors of the commercial building. A few ceiling lights scarcely illuminated the elliptical hallway. Finding no one even at the reception desk, the policeman was left with no option but to jump over the grill door and make for the stairs.

He climbed past the empty ground floor appearing to serve as an airy waiting area and nothing more. The locked-down first floor, though, piqued the cop's interest: one he'd not forget to revisit on his way back down. He climbed further up. On the second floor, Thomas found two skinny blue collars mopping the floor. He was in no mood to play a good cop. He paused for a moment, in an attempt to show them their places with a dominant face. But his subtle body language didn't seem to do things.

The workers creepily gazed back at the policemen — continuing to go about the mop job alongside. Thomas considered getting off the stairs to look for any and all absurdities he could imagine. But he kept it moving, not wanting to walk over the wet floor wearing muddy boots. Neither did he prefer to set off the seemingly short-tempered bottom-feeders. The likelihood of finding a criminal in hiding, though, seemed to shoot up with more and more such anomalies. This time around, it wasn't just the narrow-minded cop in him; something didn't sit right from the first second.

It was only on reaching the third floor he could believe the building housed a functional office. A fairly simplistic bullpen that could hold about twenty-five people was left vacant — the workday had presumably come to an end. The first unaesthetic choice gleamed from along the walls to his side: the better part of the storage space buried under a long polythene sheet. However, upon attention to detail, it didn't take long for Thomas to tell the sheets covered the old computer parts strewn about the mounted table. Something else Thomas wanted to revisit on his way back.

Mild voices echoed in the corner room. Otherwise, there was no one to make any noise. Chairs were tucked into the tables. All lights but the corner ones, plugged out. Break room and waiting area, curtained up. Windows and back doors, bolted shut. A watery scent of floor-cleaning liquid filled the air. Thomas was not up for walking into two or more strangers having a private conversation. "Hello?" He called loudly. The voices fell to a silence.

Two men dressed up in crinkled formal wear raced out, neither one leaving way for the other. One of them — fancily suited up from the necktie to under the knees — was contrastingly shoeless. Tall, black, and bald: if something were to be the polar opposite of this Biscuit the cop was out for, it was him. "Who is this?" He asked, commandingly.

Behind him stood an equally wasted gentleman; his curly gray hair, a tangled mess. Code gray hair, though. He looked about over fifty, and his face cut — quite frankly — annoying enough to don a disapproving face the bosses were known for. Thomas recognized his captain in him, and that was good enough for fleeting confirmations. With delayed relief, Thomas caught his breath, slowly reaching for the badge in his back pocket. "Detective Thomas

Lee, I'm with the Cleveland Police." He remarked for the hundredth time for the day.

"I'm sorry, is there a problem?" The bald guy continued, still holding on to the gravitas. It was as though he'd expected problems to come calling.

"I'm Jerome Biscuit. I run the Cleveland branch." The other guy suggested, kind enough to give himself up like a dear. "What can I do for you?"

"Well, um..." Thomas didn't himself know what he came looking for. "I have a couple of questions. And, you are?"

"I'm Jeff Walker. I'm the regional manager." Jeff announced, to which Thomas reacted a bit curiously, seeking to know the guy's exact job status. Gauging that rightly, he continued with added pride. "I'm second to the CEO. I take care of the logistical end of things." Thomas nodded, partly stifling an urge to take a dig at the poorly maintained working conditions to the very head of logistics. "I'm his boss." He gratuitously described, pointing at Jerome Biscuit who blatantly rolled his eyes.

"Very well. I'm talking to two important people, I might as well come out with the truth." The policeman pulled out his phone to show the photos he'd taken earlier that evening. "This is Keith Warren."

"I'm sorry I have to cut you off." It was Jeff Walker. "I have someplace to be right away." He remembered. "I was *just* preparing to leave."

"Oh." The detective was taken aback for a second. "I understand that you have important things to do, Mr.Walker. But from my perspective, you say you're gonna leave right as I show you a picture of this guy," said a quick-witted Thomas.

"Oh c'mon, this is absurd!" The regional manager barked. "Who even is this guy?" He questioned, grabbing the phone from Thomas's hands. Fair to say, the big-headed cop didn't like it one bit. "This is an emergency. For your sake, I have seen his face once, twice now. There you go, thrice." He said, drawing the mobile farther and closer to his face. "Excuse me, officer." He handed back the phone.

"Wait!" Officer Thomas Lee ordered. He flipped through a few other photos to land on the second suspect of the day. "What about him? Do you know this guy?" He shook his head even before getting to see the photo. "This is Caleb Davidson."

"No, I don't. I swear to God." He barked again. Thomas Lee didn't like a lot of people. But this guy, he hated to death. "Now, can I go?"

"Can I ask what is so urgent that you have to walk away from an investigation?"

"May I plead the fifth?" He laughed before walking away. Regardless of whether the regional manager knew things the police would like to know, Thomas couldn't bring himself to believe anybody would act so suspicious that they're practically sowing the seeds of doubt along the way. With this guy though, Thomas didn't know if he was plain bad at handling cops or actually stupid enough to be a dick about everything — to a police officer out of all people. A third option he couldn't completely glide over was that he was perhaps genius enough to leave Thomas Lee to suffer between difficult decisions.

"That's his way of being confident." Thomas heard from behind. "In case you're wondering, he's not a clown. He's only trying to show that he's confident."

"If he's so desperate to show he's got nothing to hide, maybe he does — in fact — have something to hide." Thomas suggested out loud.

Jerome Biscuit shrugged his shoulders. "I'm not hinting at anything, young man. He is my boss, don't you forget that." Biscuit seemed like a way nicer man than he'd originally come across with the bald guy in the room. "So, what's going on?"

"Oh, yeah." Thomas came forward. "He's Keith Warren. He was picked up near your offices about six weeks ago. He broke out of prison this morning. We have reason to believe that J.J.Designers has something to do with him."

"Oh... No." He went. "We are a respectable firm. We don't deal with criminals."

"What about him?" Thomas showed him the next picture. "This is Caleb Davidson." It wasn't wise to let Biscuit know Caleb was caught misappropriating his name. Moreover, from deep down, he felt Jerome Biscuit was a good man. Thomas wasn't very known for going against his gut. As most expected, Jerome Biscuit showed no signs of knowing him or having seen him before.

"Are you sure you don't know him? Cause he seems to know you." He revealed without thinking. Thomas pinched himself in the behind.

"Really?" He asked, genuinely perplexed. "How do you say that?"

"Never mind." He continued. "That's confidential... That wraps up our conversation I suppose." Lacking a clear goal in mind, Thomas had nowhere to go from there. Heck, he'd have liked it had Jeff Walker interchanged roles with the sweet old Jerome Biscuit. That could have saved him a lot of work. Jerome nodded along.

"By the way..." Thomas did a good job of not giving away the fact that he was only sitting out the entire conversation to serendipitously bring up this. "Can I get Mr.Walker's phone number?" Jerome Biscuit nodded before going for his phone as Thomas chimed in again. "Personal number. I know enough to safely say he should be having a work phone and a personal phone." He declared without doubts.

"Oh, but..." Jerome considered. "He wouldn't like that."

"Look at it this way. We might need him on the phone in the middle of the night. I call his office phone, it goes straight to voicemail." He conjectured. "We're dealing with a very sensitive matter, Mr.Biscuit." He said with a straight face. Of course, the man had to give in to Thomas Lee's demands.

• • •

It hadn't been half an hour since Thomas wanted the rookie on the Michigan Bandits, he had already changed his mind. For an excuse to hang around and wait for Theo to come back with good news,

Thomas opted to tour the place. By virtue of friendships around the department, he had scared up the perfect idea to break past the impasse he had seemingly run into. But this idea required putting Theo on the line. Happy as he was to assume the prestigious protege status, Theo jumped at the chance to track down Jeff Walker's mobile phone.

"But we don't have a warrant." He declared, a little too disciplined to succeed someone like Thomas Lee.

"If I got the warrant, would I ask you to do it for me?"

"I'll take care of it." Theo declared with gusto despite which Thomas took it upon himself to walk him through like he was some rookie. Which he was.

"Now, whom do you call to get down to cell towers?" He even quizzed him over the phone so they wouldn't get kicked out of the force the first night Thomas landed the Keith Warren case. He instead preferred for it to be the last night working the case as well. Only if there was a more reliable cop he could bank on.

"Officer Melvin."

"Right. And what else?"

"I'll have to wait until he talks to his people on the inside."

"Inside of what?"

"None of my business."

"That's my boy!" It had been quite some time until he last talked to Theodore. But he'd promised not to dial back and pester him. Having scanned every inch of the parking lot twice, he began looking for someplace else to while away the time in. It was when he remembered the strange interaction with the sketchy blue collars. But when he ran back to size them up with authority, they'd long gone home.

Thomas leaned against the handrails, closing his eyes. He'd been working overtime without a place to sit. He slowly crouched down, eyes still shut. Despite it seeming a big day, mentally laying down every single finding from the last twelve hours didn't prove jack. There was no common direction everything pointed toward. Was it all pointless random revelations? It surely didn't feel that way.

Thomas was convinced they just had to connect the dots to be done.

He'd already decided he wasn't gonna go home until the case was solved. But he'd undermined the magic of a good night's sleep. Regardless, what's decided is decided. If not until he solves the case, he reckoned he could work at least until he blacks out and topples over. From a position to fall asleep if unbothered for a while, Thomas quickly got on his feet and continued walking. Walking seemed to be the only way to keep up with reality.

He slapped on the lights he could find since darkness brought sleep to him. Attempting to go back in time, he recollected every feeling of his from about thirty minutes before. He stormed into rooms he found to be suspicious and ripped apart curtains he found to be concealing. Next, on the first floor, he dashed himself against chairs and tables, navigating to the switchboard in the dark. Slowly but surely, he'd lit up half the building, quite contradictory to what was usually done at this time of the day.

No doors opened came to his rescue. Sometime or the other, Jerome Biscuit was gonna walk in on him. He had to make reasons for going crazy. Else, he'd risk letting people think he'd gone crazy. He closed one door after another, running around in a frenzy. As he pushed away an already closed door, he understood he never opened it in the first place. He couldn't. The door had been locked from the inside. From when he walked past the locked-down floor, it was the doubt in his mind that kept him running. The exact doubt that came knocking for the second time now.

Thomas dropped himself over the door. As anyone barely sensible could say, he did no damage. He kicked the door. He jumped at it, pushed it, and kicked it again. Compared to what the surroundings suggested, the door seemed significantly stronger than the rest. Did he try and validate his hunch? No, he tried even harder to break open the door that could possibly hold all the answers he'd been looking for. Possibly, being the word to remember. "Aah!" He yelled at the top of his lungs and ran toward the door, before he sprung off of it, landing on his back. He curled into a ball, he'd finally lost himself to the moody night.

"Thomas?" Jerome came running. He'd gone mad for the judgmental eyes of his very suspect to see. "What is going on here?" Amidst the cluttered mess, he lay as one among the many inanimate subjects.

"Open the door, open the door." He muttered, seemingly back from a brain freeze. "The door." He repeated, pointing to somewhere away from the door in question.

"It's the store room! What is your problem, man?" For the first time in a while, Jerome Biscuit was the only one making sense. "I've been waiting for you to get done. Didn't think you were doing this in the name of police work. It's late already, who's gonna clean up this mess?" Thomas gradually reached for the tabletop, standing back up without motivation. "Are you even a cop?" Biscuit questioned.

"What?" The policeman wasn't in his element. "I am a cop. I didn't say that already?"

"I'm calling 911."

"I *am* 911." Thomas cried. "No. I just-" He stuttered. "I didn't sleep last night." He bent down to pick up his pocket note. "Or the night before, or the night before."

"What's behind this door? You tell me!" Biscuit shouted. Thomas shook his head, breathing heavily. He had also dropped his pen, his wallet, and about everything but his badge and gun, which he held on to, like dear life.

"See, I'm a cop." He bent down again, on the verge of falling down for a concussion. "It's the store room, I remember now. I'd already gone through its back door. See, the front door was locked from the inside. I saw that with my own eyes. I..." He dragged. "... I think I forgot." Biscuit pulled him back up,

"Get the fuck out of here." He picked up the copper's belongings for him. Among many other things Thomas had littered the floors with, was a plastic bag. "Get out." Biscuit pushed the young man, handing him the bag of things. Thomas walked out with a cigarette in his mouth. Thankfully, he hadn't dropped the keys to his ride.

CHAPTER XVI

D-Day

When they'd utterly run out of cash, Cody and Devon decided to go after their boss Jerome Biscuit. They were three weeks away from D-Day, and out there counting stacks from Jerome's wallet. Such side quests only furthered their confidence that they still had it in them. From the day they disposed of their guns in Saginaw, they had successfully kept themselves off ammunition. But they had also promised to walk away from violent crimes: something they couldn't quite keep up. Coming from beating henchmen to oblivion though, a hand-knife situation wasn't exactly what they called a violent crime.

They had successfully lived without Keith or his money for three months now. And, he had contacted them, wishing for a meeting. It had been quite a while since they last talked. More than anyone, Cody wanted them to go back the way they were. He even considered letting him in on the plans. But how could they enrich an already enriched mind? Keith stormed into the room with a different plan.

Failing to catch the look on his face, they rose from their seats smiling gleefully. Their ex-partner had come in to meet them after so long. "What do you think of yourselves?" He came yelling. "Who allowed you to make big fucking plans?" The good old Michael, half hard of hearing, had somehow blurted out everything to Keith. "That's right. I visited Michael at the hospital. What do you think you're doing?" He grabbed Cody's shirt collar.

"I was just about to tell you." Cody calmly responded, throwing his hands above his head. "And... nice to meet you, too." He added.

"Don't play with me!" Keith screamed. Devon nudged the angry lad back for defense. "Why are you still in the city?" He then questioned.

"I can be anywhere I want." Devon responded, taking the question personally.

"We made promises. No more crimes." His voice cracked.

"But then, what did you do? Called us out for begging to you. We don't depend on you anymore." Devon asserted. Cody stepped back, disappointed at the turn of events.

"If you get caught..." Keith raised his voice. "... You put me in danger! If I get caught, who's there for my mother?" This time around, he had familial emotions backing his anger. Devon and Keith stared eye-to-eye, ready for a face-off.

"Look, guys." Cody said submissively, driving the two apart. He wasn't about to fend for his ego in a room with Ledger and Warren. "We need money to move wherever it is that we're moving to." He told Keith. "If you can give us a hundred thousand dollars, we'll drop the plan and get out of your hair. If not... Don't stop us."

"What if you get caught?"

"We won't!" Cody exclaimed. "It's our office, did Michael tell you that?" He nodded insincerely. "So, come with us." Cody remarked indifferently. Devon let out a controlled growl at his friend. Not controlled enough though.

"Devon wouldn't like me there." Keith declared, giving him the side-eye. It was his fear of feeling unwelcome that dissuaded him. Not that he was hurt at all by the breaking of promises. Ledger didn't deny his claims.

"I'll deal with him. Help us win, we'll leave right away." Cody said.

"I want a chunk of that money." Inside his head, Keith only agreed since he wanted them out of his life. He wasn't ready to accept that he had just agreed to take part in a crime. Claude would kill herself if she came to hear of it. Now was the time Cody had to side with Devon. But he didn't think about how Devon would react. For the sake of old friendships, he agreed to shake on it. Ledger left the room speaking no words.

"I'll honor my end. You honor yours. Say something doesn't go according to plan, you'll be the one paying the price." Keith warned, not an ounce grateful for his old mate's attempts to kill the monotony in his life. He bid farewell, slapping Cody's cheeks to have some fun of his own. Cody closed his eyes, not losing his patience. One has to think straight when the other doesn't. Upon the guest's departure, the two friends reconciled.

• • •

It was D-Day. Cody Mills and Devon Ledger packed up their desks as the clocks struck six. When the CEO didn't care about dysfunctional cameras, it was already a sign something was off. Only after weeks of skimming around, they were sure there wasn't a single working camera inside Jenson's office. The dummy camera Jenson placed to blend in with the rest was replaced by a replica they'd bought with Biscuit's money.

They'd only stayed for a few months. But if they didn't mess up the math, Jenson opened his vault every two months. They'd singled out two different days six weeks apart, either one of them good for the operation. It had been a week since Jenson last opened his vault. Whatever the day, it had to be done before he even considered opening it again. Thanks to Keith Warren, they had to rush things and pick the first day they found interesting.

They egressed the building with the buzzing crowd only to never pass through the gates again that night. They had picked an entrance of their choice, having mastered the art of jumping over compound walls. A six-foot wall separated J.J.Designers from the textile mill around the corner. Keith was asked to wait right there wearing a rucksack full of tools of the day.

For the past few weeks, the three of them met every night at the same spot, discussing strategies. Cody and Devon had to wait every time as a strange red vehicle dropped off Keith Warren. None of their questions were answered.

Along the way, Cody recollected everything he'd learned in preparation. Jenson had locked all the money in the hidden storage space. Inside the general-purpose vault his office housed, he had someone build a second vault, the second one entirely hidden from view. Only from the security cameras, they couldn't learn as much as they wanted to. Yet, they knew enough to safely say the bossman had stacked up quite a lot of banknotes.

As the sun went down, Cody and Devon trespassed against the law. Keith did not say yes to coming in with them. He wanted to play the game as safely as he could. He stood watch, waiting for them to come back with all the money in the world. Things did not go as planned though.

• • •

The two friends ran back and forth from the ground to the top. They had successfully broken through all the obstacle courses they had planned on running into. When Devon danced his way to the treasure trove with a duffel bag in his hands, he'd realized they were fucked.

They never planned on wiping the case clean, raising suspicion. All they wanted was a few grands that could help them move. But the duffel bag did no good. Not one bit of that cash was worth a thousand dollars each, worth a hundred each, not even goddamn ten. Daniel Jenson had filled up his extravagant vault with George goddamn Washingtons. A duffel bag full of one-dollar bills would amount to less than the money they'd robbed off Jerome in the parking lot. From their years of experience, only an absolute moron would hoard one-dollar bills. Well, in this case, a bloody genius.

They had wasted months on this operation. Devon twitched in fear. So close were they to the end line, that they didn't think anything could possibly deter them from the course. Cody waddled up the stairs groaning loudly. Ledger rushed to shush him. He was found balancing a three-foot-tall cylinder, wading through the dark. As Devon lent a helping hand, they carefully placed it on the floor. "Where did you find this?" Devon whispered.

"On the ground floor." Cody declared. "Let's wipe the case clean." The two friends moved eight red cylindrical tubs up and down for three floors. What looked to be a thirty-minute job came to be a three-hour one. Despite multiple calls from Keith Warren, they were fixated on the moment and its joy. That, paired with an adrenaline rush of not knowing if someone would walk out the door at that moment, the night showed them what they had been missing out on.

Keith didn't understand why they were asking him to stay around for hours until they returned. By the time they realized the boxes were too heavy to transport without a vehicle, it was already 3:00 a.m. The money had to be stashed within the confines of J.J.Designers. Devon broke open the locked-down warehouse to find a temporary home for the money. They had to hold everything and wait until the next time it was safe enough to go out and about at midnight.

If at all Jenson opened his vault before the money was out, he'd only know that the money was gone. He'd neither know where to look for nor whom to ask for. According to the office calendar, the next time the office was gonna be empty was six weeks away.

It wasn't until half past three when Cody sprinted back to where Keith had been camping, waiting for the two to get back. Cody had stuffed the duffel bag with whatever money they couldn't fit into the boxes. If worse came to worst, they'd at least walk home with a grand at best. He flung the duffel bag to the other side of the wall and sprinted back into J.J.Designers. Keith was asked to hold on for a few more minutes.

There's no way he could have ever foreseen what was coming. To his eyes, everything had been going as per the plan. Until Cody Mills dialed him up. "If you say my name to the cops, if you say Devon's name to the cops, Mrs.Claude will die. Be smart and save your mother." He warned and hung up the next second. He was disgusted by his own words.

Cody Mills had planted a bag of cocaine inside the duffel bag. Keith didn't dream of it. Only because he was disrespectful, the two friends decided to show him they'd not gone soft just yet. After all, they were used to beating up innocent people for a living. Why not a guilty man? Ever since they moved to Cleveland, their former friend was nothing short of an annoyance. They'd been forever wanting to humble him, and it had all mounted up to this. The police soon arrived.

When the two friends ripped off Jerome Biscuit for some money, Jeff Walker was sure they weren't merely first-timers. Only a man no stranger to violence could think about such stuff, he'd assumed. Watching them from a distance that night, he promised himself he wasn't gonna let them walk away happily. Not because he cared about Biscuit, but because he hated their guts. He'd been observing every step of theirs. Wanting to exact his revenge, but not knowing how to was a position he despised to stay at.

When they came back to get Daniel Jenson, he'd understood it was his time to pounce. He was neither an outlaw nor a member of some chain gang. He was the nobody they aspired to be. Considering that he wasn't about to buck up and go on the field himself, he had to wait another six weeks to catch them red-handed. And, maybe also take home some of the cash for personal use.

CHAPTER XVII

Tracked

Officer Thomas Lee was driving home at full speed. He'd never been embarrassed by a civilian before, forget an office manager he hadn't ever met. As much as he'd have liked it to go back and exercise his power over Jerome Biscuit, he was a little too sleep-deprived to retrace his path. He had to fall asleep and forget about Keith Warren to be back at it the next morning. All he feared was falling asleep at the wheel in lethargy.

His phone rang. "Who's ready to hear some good news?" Thomas couldn't even pretend to level with Theo's passion.

"What is it?" He asked, devoid of any excitement. The rookie worked his way through the negative air around Thomas who wasn't half as animated — as anyone could say. Particularly Theo, having spoken so many calls to Thomas that very day. He still had to report his progress before personal questions.

"I've tracked down your man." He announced and fell silent. Theo assumed his news had to do some good in raising the man's spirit. If not, he wasn't gonna proceed at all.

"Yeah?" Thankfully, Thomas sounded better than before. Though, not as zealous. He rubbed his eyes, one hand still on the steering wheel. "Where is he?"

"I can't precisely pinpoint him for you... But you know that." He declared, taking it further. "He's in the far east. At the very least, twenty miles from J.J.Designers."

Thomas cornered his police car on recognizing people frowning at a policeman on the phone while driving. He wasn't on the highway anymore. "Theo, I've come close to my home. That's too far."

"But you asked me to get it done!" He remarked out of vexation. The rookie remembered he had to calm down. "Thomas, why didn't you wait? Tracking down a guy takes an hour or more. You know that, don't you?" He asked all the right questions while managing to hold onto a collected disposition. Thomas could rage at no one but himself. He chose to stay mute rather than apologize.

"Hello?" The copper heard a different voice. How relieved he was, that he plunged at the opportunity to speak before Theo came back on.

"Susanne, is that you?" Thomas asked.

"That's me. I brought Fletcher along. Theodore called me saying you didn't trust the night-shifters. Since everyone's working, I figured I might as well join the team."

"So that you know, I thought of surprising you with them." Theodore had plucked the phone to dish out the angst.

"I'm sorry, Theo." He owned up to his mistake: something he doesn't do often.

"Do you remember me?" Thomas heard a third voice. Having to deal with so many people while half-asleep was enough to wake him up.

"I'm sorry again, Justin." He had abandoned his partner at the convenience store only to never think of picking him up again. Since Thomas last talked to him about the video footage, he had comfortably purged his partner off his memory. All he could think about was himself and the case he had worked so much for. "I'm being too kind, aren't I?" He mumbled quietly as images of his previous interactions flashed over his head.

"We're working on the Michigan Bandits, Tom." Susanne indulged. "Fletcher and I." She said, giving credit to the unluckiest man of the lot. "No luck so far."

"But..." Fletcher chimed in, as rehearsed. Seeing the rookie hate himself for getting screamed in the first week, Susanne reckoned she could help him earn back a little respect. It was commendable they had dug up dirt on the name in an hour's time. "We found an online presence. From a few months ago. Right here in Cleveland."

"Going by the same name." Susanne added. Fletcher couldn't even speak the written phrase, she thought. He nodded curiously.

Thomas jumped out of his car. "Are you serious?" It was enough motivation for him to forget the past and become a night-shifter for the day. "They have the address included?"

"It's geotagged." Fletcher stated confidently. "They might not have meant it, but geotagged photos give away your location." For once, Thomas Lee trusted Fletcher without second thoughts. He was speaking Thomas's language.

"This Michigan Bandit, Thomas. Is there solid proof..." Susanne questioned.

"I think we should check it out." Thomas cut her off. "Right away."

"We'll take care of it." Theo remarked urgently. "You check out your guy's last known location, Thomas." The detective acquiesced. Given that the others followed the newfound lead, Thomas had no option but to go check on Jeff Walker.

"Are you sure you're good?" Susanne asked. "Take Justin with you, maybe." He denied all second-hand inputs. Thomas Lee was more sure than ever that the Michigan Bandits were the answer to everything. Except this time when it mattered the most, he wasn't the man. Everybody but him was off to find answers while he had to go after a regional manager.

Thomas passed out that evening. He'd apologized to people. He'd cried to himself, he'd even played games with an old lady. It was a day for new experiences. And for once, it was okay for him to give up the central spot.

The cops had closed in on Jeff Walker's location within a one-mile radius. Within the perimeter though, there seemed to exist not more than three residential quarters. Of which, two were separate houses. Going by Theo's hunch, if Jeff wasn't stranded in the middle of a wasteland, the only other place left out was a lonely apartment building. Thomas pressed down the accelerator for a long ride.

CHAPTER XVIII

Blowout

Cody Mills, Devon Ledger, Jeff Walker, Daniel Jenson, and now Keith Warren. For owning the smallest home, Cody had to receive an unhealthy number of guests. Seeing Keith outside of a jail cell was another shocker they didn't have enough time to react to. At the entrance of Cody's apartment, Keith pulled out a brand-new gun from his pockets. But, Daniel had two of them. Three, counting Jeff's, from inside the bag. Nobody asked for a fifth person to join the hunt.

"Who the hell are you?" Jenson asked.

"I called you this morning." Keith replied coldly. Jenson nodded as though Keith didn't just allude to having known the bossman earlier. The two friends sighed at once, not quite the appropriate reaction. They'd already seen one too many surprises, they were ready to see dead people alive by then. Jeff, on the other hand, seemed very uninterested in the proceedings. "Can we go inside and talk? We don't want anyone to overhear us." Keith said, holding the gun still.

It took him six weeks to summon up the courage and break out of Rodger's Penitentiary. The last thing looming over his head was the one-sided phone conversation with Cody Mills. He'd been waking up every day from a nightmare. Sitting inside a rotten jail cell, he had no control over the outside world. He'd been cultivating a murderous rage. When he told off Cody and Devon, it was only the latter nudging him and fighting back. He remembered Cody simply standing back, wearing a disappointed look. Keith had taken him for a gentleman. Knowing them for years — though scarcely — he couldn't accept that he tried to help out people who framed each other for revenge.

Thanks to the friends he'd made in those three months away from his gang, he didn't die on his way out of the forest he passed through. Caleb Davidson was much more of an acquaintance than Cody or Devon had ever been. It was possibly the first time in his adulthood he'd met someone who wasn't from a gang. Caleb drove around Keith in his car any time of the day. He was ready to drop him off at shady locations and pick him up when he was done. He was ready to buy him instant noodles at midnight, and he was ready to drive him home butt-naked the day he broke out of prison. All he expected was the unfiltered truth in return.

But Keith hadn't even gifted him with the one thing he'd asked for. The day he broke out of Rodgers was the day he realized he was Cody in Caleb's world. It took a weight off his chest when he came clean to Caleb. Upon hearing the unvarnished truth, he was even more ready to take risks for his friend.

"He called you?" Devon had to question the bossman. It didn't seem wise to directly ask the man how they'd let him go from jail.

"I did." Keith interjected. "Going by the office calendar you showed me, last night was your one chance at getting the money home." He said, nearing Cody Mills. "I was ready to escape the day before. Couldn't control my nerves. I peed my pants at the last moment." He revealed. "But I just knew I had to break out. If not, I'd hate myself for it." Cody moved backward. "Since I'm going to prison anyway, I might as well do something to deserve it."

When his mother didn't believe he was set up, he tortured himself for nights. It was a no-brainer she was gonna freak out on seeing him. He couldn't completely look past the possibility that she would call the cops herself. But it had to be done for him to function again. For him to fulfill his purpose. Once out of prison, he swiftly navigated to Caleb's car as already planned. Until he personally confirmed his mum wasn't killed, he didn't bat an eyelid.

He attempted to train his mother one last time since the police were gonna pay her a visit sometime or the other. On seeing her son again, her happy half had lost to his persuasive words. Just for the day, he'd appointed Caleb Davidson for her security. As he kissed her goodbye before leaving, he'd checked off everything he had to do before he set off to never come back again. He'd been forever yearning to go against Cody's cold-hearted warning.

"As soon as I could, I called him." He elaborated to prove a point that he wasn't ill-witted. "I told him about the garage. I told him about the plan. I told him what shitty people you were."

"But, when I asked you who you were, you hung up the phone." Jenson interrupted, giving him a suspicious look. The bossman had to naturally doubt everything and everyone coming his way. Who would voluntarily wanna speak to Daniel Jenson?

"I had to. Somehow, I wondered if there was a chance I'd walk away without revenge." He introspected. "Deep down, I knew I'd be there to put a bullet in your heads." Keith put his second hand over the gun, squarely aiming at Cody Mills.

"No!" Daniel Jenson shrieked, reminding the housemates of the two guns he was holding onto. "Show me the money first." He declared. Jeff Walker was trapped in a place he wasn't a part of. Because he owned a gun license, he'd reckoned it would be a ride to scare a bunch of seemingly vulnerable lowlives. He wasn't ever gonna use his gun. He wasn't ever gonna hurt someone. If not for eyeing the bossman's position, he wouldn't have voluntarily offered to visit a deathly wounded Jenson. He had his inherent greed to point hands at — over every other thing.

"Show me the money." Jenson repeated, loud enough to startle the lot. Cody didn't dare to meet his eye. He looked around for answers. Keith pulled back to let the man get back his money. He wasn't about the money anymore. "The money!" Jenson yelled, now turning to Devon. Neither did he have an answer that could save the two from a bad ending. He looked straight at Cody to save himself.

"What did you do with the money?" Keith questioned, striking Mills at his chest lightly. He had to send away the people he didn't want to see dead. Now that he'd come all this way, his hands were itching to pull the trigger. He couldn't let the passage of time soothe his wrath. "Where's the money?"

"It's not here." Devon muttered.

"What?" Jenson howled in the loudest voice. "What the fuck?" He advanced rapidly, clenching his teeth. Neither could he kill them nor could he leave them be. He couldn't punch them, for his hands were full. He couldn't put the gun away, for there was a second gunman in the room. It took a decade's work to make it and not a day to rob it. Only the sight of money could calm him down. He was beginning to go numb with rage. "Aah!"

Keith pulled the slider, ready to fire. "Don't you dare!" Jenson screamed. Devon held his ears in terror. "I need the money now!" Saliva rolled down his mouth without him realizing it. His eyes had turned red.

"I can take you there!" Cody yelled back.

"Stop fucking lying!" He was on his way to pull the trigger himself. If not for the money, the room would be dead meat by now. "How much more should I wait to get back the money that I earned?" He kicked Devon noncommittally, the man had to have someone to beat up. Keith raised his hands again, words helped him no more. "If you shoot him, I'll shoot you!" Jenson exclaimed. "I need the money now!"

"Devon lives on the other side." Cody let him know.

"Of course, he fucking does." He claimed, heavy on the irony. "What do you think of me?" He aimed one of his guns at Cody, trying his best not to lose his nerves. Jeff Walker thought he was smart to subtly reach for his bags. He looked up and down to ensure the same. Jenson — with all focus on the two friends — wasn't that big a multitasker. To see through the anger was his first priority.

With a grin on his face, Jeff looked up one last time. He froze. Keith caught the regional manager searching for his gun with trembling hands. The room fell silent for a millisecond. Jeff ended up helping ease off some tension, offering himself up like that. "Who *is* this guy?" Keith wondered.

"Let me go." Jeff mumbled.

"Aren't you the mastermind?" Jenson claimed with a smirk.

"He isn't." Keith quickly responded. Jeff violently shook his head. Devon gradually allowed himself to breathe. Jenson shifted his eyes left and right. "I don't even know him." Keith added. Jenson turned to Cody, producing a mechanical laugh. Laughing at himself seemed to help him from pulling the trigger.

"So, you lied about this too?" He laughed harder. "And you had him convinced I was dying?" Harder. "I'm the biggest fool, aren't I?" Keith was on his watch, ready to go off at any moment necessary. A gun suddenly popped up from behind. Keith threw himself at the wall. Jenson slipped to the ground to save himself. Cody was right in the range, he had to make peace with God in half a second. Jeff pulled the trigger.

The regional manager had forgotten to cock the revolver before going for it.

Keith pulled the trigger. Off, went the gun. Blood puddled the apartment tiles. The noise was multiple times louder than he'd imagined. It had been a while since Cody and Devon last heard a gunshot. Jeff fell to the floor, the bullet had perfectly pierced through his head. Daniel began producing unintelligible noises at the graphic sight. His life was never gonna be the same anymore. He was the only man left around who hadn't murdered people. For him to continue living though, that had to change.

In the next fifteen seconds, Detective Thomas Lee fired the second shot of the night at the doorknob. He had been waiting behind the door for backup. All of his partners had wandered off to a different location in search of the darned Michigan Bandits.

There was no one to convince Thomas Lee he'd been lied to. If there ever happened to be a *Michigan Bandits*, its main men were only a few feet apart from the detective. Like with almost everyone, he had taken Mrs.Claude for a fool. It didn't once cross his mind that her son might have trained her to deal with rude policemen. A geotagged image from the internet was all it took to make him look the other way. Thomas was the man responsible for a four-member squad squandering valuable time searching for something immaterial. After all, no gang would be dumb enough to call themselves the Michigan Bandits.

Thomas had just heard a gunshot. He could no longer rely on a backup team that hadn't made it yet. Jeff Walker was lying in a pool of blood: his brain poured onto the floor. Thomas looked away, stifling a gag reflex. He fleeted backward, taking cover. He'd spotted a pistol and a revolver from a second-long glance. Voices couldn't do justice. Neither could feelings. The copper had to see for himself. Sadly enough, Thomas Lee couldn't even smile to himself for finding Keith Warren.

Jenson fired towards the door. He might not have killed a person before, but he'd reckoned the night made him ready. Cody ducked down. He could see the TV cabinet within his reach. Thomas could hurt no civilian. He shot the fish tank in his view. Glass shattered everywhere, as the water flooded the living room. It was a jumpscare effective enough to throw the bossman off his course. Keith — although aghast — knew his firearm was his only companion. He couldn't see clearly. But he didn't drop the weapon at any cost. If need be, he was prepared to begin firing in all directions.

Ledger picked up the gun Jenson had dropped by accident. Nobody went for the revolver floating alongside Jeff's mushed-up tissues. Keith crawled to the corner desperately. It was too late for Daniel to realize he wasn't ready to kill a man yet.

Thomas fired again, hitting off the target purposefully. It was the most he could do, wearing a police badge. He began considering shooting down every one of them in the name of self-defense. "I'm Detective Thomas Lee." He shouted from the other side since he had to. He didn't know what he'd expected to happen on saying that. "Fuck it." He claimed to himself and gripped the gun. "No, no, no." He couldn't do that to the police job that had kept him alive.

How did Thomas miss this? A schoolboy standing in the shooting range. A stoned woman climbed down from above. The neighbors had been peeping out, on the verge of breaking down. The house opposite, luckily, had been padlocked. Civilians began flooding the floor on hearing what seemed to be gunshots. Reasonably so. As newer ones climbed up and down, the ones already there rushed back to their homes. A couple of them remained standing, no matter what. "Clear the place!" Thomas roared. "Active shooters are inside! Get out, you idiots!" Chaos further arose. This time, a much-needed one.

A minute-long recuperation time provided the shooters enough and more advantage. "Give me my money back!" Daniel cried, literally. Since he'd had no one to trust, he began wailing at everyone. Cody opened the TV cabinet: the red shoe box. He knew what he was doing. He'd last checked the box only the previous night after the falling out with Ledger.

Keith aimed squarely at Cody Mills. No matter who'd killed the fun, Keith had to reach the finish line. He had already taken a shot and wasn't gonna rest without killing his old mates. As he brought himself to pull the trigger at Cody's beautiful face, a bullet zipped through the air around his untorn face. The CEO of J.J.Designers crashed into the wall, holding his heart. Devon had fired a bullet after months. He'd finally felt like himself again. Cody rushed inside with the red box in his hand. Thomas Lee had had enough. He ran through the main door as the bedroom door closed before his eyes. Keith had pulled the trigger. For the second time in a row, he was on point.

Keith smiled. It was Devon Ledger for his second shot. He was good to check off one of the two remaining squares. Officer Thomas Lee locked eyes with Keith Warren as the dying Daniel Jenson breathed for the last time on his lap. Keith flicked the man to the floor and wiped his pants. Devon Ledger had killed a man again. He'd always feared he was gonna die a wuss he had made out of himself. Funnily enough, he felt the most alive two seconds before dying. He proudly wore the bullet as he fell to death with fulfillment.

Half of everything to the cop's eyes was either covered in glass, water, or blood. Keith Warren was covered in all three. "Drop the gun." Thomas ordered, looking straight into the runner's eyes. For one thing, he could look nowhere else for his own safety. For another, the entire house had been painted red.

"I have to kill another guy, officer." Keith responded, unhinged.

"Drop the gun. You're making a mistake."

"Guess what, I've already made one. You can't kill me, can you?" He asked maniacally.

"I can say you co-operated." Thomas tried.

"Fuck co-operation. Fuck you." Thomas moved towards his right without losing his control over Keith Warren. On his way over, he might have walked over innards and blood. Couldn't look down to confirm. He reached the closed bedroom door and knocked it with his foot.

"Go away!" He heard a man from the inside. "I'll shoot you. I have a gun. Go away!" He obviously couldn't figure out who it was from just his voice. His phone rang. Keith sneered at him, challenging the cop to answer his phone and not lose balance on the other side. It could be the backup asking for address. It could be Justin with some news. It could be Theo. It could be his captain. Thankfully, he didn't have a girlfriend. Officer Thomas Lee couldn't afford to reach into his pant pockets, putting his life on the line. "Get out of here!" He heard from the inside. Thomas could say the man was in tears inside.

"Is it Caleb?" He asked Keith, expecting him to act surprised. Keith Warren did not lose his devilish sneer. "Is it Caleb inside? Answer me." He stared down the policeman, giving him no room to let loose. Detective Thomas Lee — stuck between a ringing phone, a jailbreaker, and a nameless gunman out of sight — couldn't make a sound decision.

Epilogue

Who's Caleb? That wasn't important. The red-colored show box saved my ass. I pulled out the gun and pointed it from an angle toward the door. I cried a river. I shit my pants. Seems like I wasn't ready for death yet. But where did a policeman come from? From what I overheard, the man seemed to know Keith Warren.

Devon made no sounds. He should have died probably. But again, the monk that he was, it was possible he was only staying quiet. Keith told the cop he had one more to kill. I was alive. Did he kill Devon? I obviously couldn't have saved him had I tried. I didn't even try, though. I wiped my tears and collected myself. Crying is for the weak.

We shouldn't have moved to Cleveland. We shouldn't have chosen J.J.Designers. We definitely shouldn't have come back for the money. It was all rookie mistakes. I struck my head against the wall. I couldn't get myself to say that we shouldn't have framed that son of a bitch. But prisons are too privileged for him. He deserves to die an uglier death.

I think I got it. We should have gone in guns blazing and robbed a jewelry shop or a bank. How hard could it be? We'd messed up, going off-brand. We're not nobodies. We're not white collars. We're not fit to work a nine-to-five job. Like Daniel Jenson did, like Jeff Walker did, we pretended to be someone we weren't. The only way I'm similar to Cody Mills is I'm as poor. We had the money in our hands and we struck out.

I heard sirens around the building. I swear I could even hear swarms of people running around. I will die at a time and place of my choice. I wasn't gonna die like this. I heard a gunshot from outside. Keith Warren and the policeman: someone had shot the other. The door was gonna be opened sometime or the other. I had to be quick.

The wall. The wall behind my ancestral wardrobe.

The paint coated onto the wall hidden behind the wardrobe had broken down to particles. My pistachio green had faded so badly the wall looked half-white. Visible cracks ran through everywhere from inside, no doubt a few strong kicks were all it would have taken to break the wall down.

How could I forget the wall five feet to my right? We hadn't placed the wardrobe back into position. Before we could, Devon raged and kicked me in the shin. There was enough space for me to take position and kick down the wall. Anybody could break down my bedroom door at any moment. I kicked the wall. Once, twice, thrice.

I cannot die. I wanna live. I stepped back. Death loomed closer with every passing second. I sent myself careening into the wall with all my might. I crashed into it, falling down to the floor. The gunshot need not have been from a man to man. Keith could shoot into the air. So could the policeman. I could see only black. I couldn't move. I felt cold blood dripping from my head. I couldn't move, I couldn't speak, I couldn't cry for help. I had given myself a concussion. After all, the wall wasn't breakable.

www.ingramcontent.com/pod-product-compliance
Lightning Source LLC
LaVergne TN
LVHW041219150826
845673LV00001B/453